Wild Meddow

With a small herd of cattle and a big pack of trouble, the man known as Burt Lane rode into Northern Wyoming.

Outside the town of Clayburn, the cattle ranch known as Wild Meddow had lain untended and overgrown for many years. With no apparent lawful owner, its water and fertile soil were of much interest to the covetous Cole Dodgson and Vaughn Maber.

When they eventually decide to overrun the ranch, Burt Lane must declare his real identity. Then, when his friend Hester Brax is taken hostage, he decides that the time for long-awaited retribution has arrived.

By the same author

Glass Law
The Evil Star
Run Wild
The Black Road
Wolf Meat
Yellow Dog
Cold Guns
Big Greasewood
Blood Legs
The Goose Moon
Miller's Ride
The Rosado Gang
The Iron Roads
Lizard Wells
Hoke John's Land

Wild Meddow

Caleb Rand

A Black Horse Western

ROBERT HALE · LONDON

© Caleb Rand 2010
First published in Great Britain 2010

ISBN 978-0-7090-8875-2

Robert Hale Limited
Clerkenwell House
Clerkenwell Green
London EC1R 0HT

www.halebooks.com

Typeset by
Derek Doyle & Associates, Shaw Heath
Printed and bound in Great Britain by
CPI Antony Rowe, Chippenham and Eastbourne

1

In the northern Wyoming cow town of Clayburn, outside of the Fallen Drummer Saloon, several hitched ponies bore the brand of the Ankle Iron ranch. Others carried the mark of Red Ribbon or Single Rig. It was a wild, cattlemen's drink hole, and Burton Lane crabbed his roan mare across the mud ruts, further along the street.

There were fewer customers at Lefty Detes. Two men were sitting at a table, drinking and playing penny ante poker, three more were standing near one end of the bar. Burt walked towards them, but stopped alongside a cloth-covered platter. The bartender placed a mug of gravy sop and two corn dodgers on to the bar, then a bottle of whiskey and a glass. Burt nodded, turned half-interested to the testy exchange ahead of him.

Fraser Brax, editor of the *Clayburn Tidings* was angry, but evidently not with his companions. It was plain they'd all been quarrelling for some time, and the newspaperman had a head of steam going.

'Before long, this range is goin' to be soaked in blood,' he insisted. 'When folk start their recriminatin', just remember it was me who warned of it.'

'Agh, it ain't much more'n badgerin', an' that ain't against the law just yet,' one of the other men said.

It was only when the man moved to pick up his glass that Burt saw the silver star of a county sheriff, pinned to the lapel of his coat.

'I can only do somethin' when there's actual violence, an' so far, there ain't been none, so don't you go printin' otherwise,' Sheriff Warner Herrick continued.

'For Chris'sakes, Sheriff, you ever heard o' headin' 'em off? Both factions are gatherin', an' even a witlin' can see there's another war brewin'. An' most likely, right here in town,' Brax aired his fearful annoyance.

'Well, I hadn't yet reckoned myself as the town's half-bake,' Herrick said tolerantly. 'Anyways, you got a competent marshal in Grif, here. What makes you think the sheepmen are lookin' for a home in this neck o' the woods? Everythin's owned an' occupied. Specially along Gray Bull Creek. They try grabbin' anythin' there an' they'll have a brace o' US marshals *an'* me landin' on 'em.'

Burt took a mouthful of dunked dodger, gave the barman another nod and took a refill.

'Personally, I don't give a tinker's cuss for either

side if they start a fight.' The sheriff was pursuing his take on the situation. 'But if they *do*, my concern will be for them settlers, 'cause they'll be caught, plum center. If the sheepmen and cattlemen hire gunnies, *they* know what to expect . . . what's comin' to 'em. Shame is, all the farmers are concerned about's milk, taters an' beans, but it's *them*, that's payin' taxes.'

'When Maber and Dodgson move in, they've schemed up a way for the law to support 'em,' Brax responded quickly.

'You figure on Brew Carron, or the Pooles sellin' their range land? Why, they wouldn't sell a quart o' cow's belly gas to a *sheepman*,' Herrick countered. 'So how you figure it's goin' to be done lawfully?'

'By comin' through the old Wild Meddow range, that's how. It's land that ain't occupied, an' there's nothin' an' nobody to stop 'em.'

At the mention of Wild Meddow, Burt's jaw gritted for the shortest moment. The two law officers exchanged a look of mild concern.

'Does anyone know, who *does* own that Wild Meddow ground?' Grif Pruett asked.

Brax shook his head. 'Word was that someone bought it off a beneficiary of Conrad Meddow. But that was a few years back. If the sheepmen get on to it, you won't want to be lookin' for any title papers. It'll be the Sheridan courts that have to decide what happens, an' that's more'n a hundred miles up an' over the Bighorns.'

They continued their crotchety discussion, were

still at it when, ten minutes later, a small group of tough-looking men, pushed their way through the batwings. The conversations ceased, the card players held their game and the barman removed the whiskey bottle from the counter. Burt cursed and drily congratulated himself on the timing of his arrival.

Two of the men walked purposefully to within six feet of Burt and stood either side of him. From their reflections in the back bar mirror, Burt recognized them both as having been stood watching from the sidewalk, when he'd rode into town.

The shortest man started his broad, meaty jowls working. 'We met somewhere?' he rumbled out. 'I sort o' got a gift for faces.'

With a look of casual disinterest, Burt studied his second corn dodger, then he gave a wry smile. With a gift for faces, the man should be *telling*, not asking. He pushed his empty glass across the bar for another refill, but it wasn't a move intended to necessarily shut the man up.

'Hey, I'm speakin' to you,' the meaty-faced man continued truculently. 'You sidin' with the cattlemen around here? Employed by 'em, maybe?'

Burt turned to face the man. He shook his head and gave an icy smile. 'Neither,' he said, 'if it's any business o' yours.'

The other man saw the impending danger for his colleague and butted in. 'My name's Vaughn Maber,' he said. 'We're runnin' some big flocks into the valley. Rush here's a mite proddy over cowmen's hired guns.'

'I'm sure he's proddy over a lot o' things,' Burt said, shortly. 'But I ain't a hired gun to *cow* men or any other kind.'

'Just who *are* you, feller?' Marshal Pruett asked, having noted Burt's gun belt and what looked like a serviceable Colt. 'Can't be too sure, in these troubled times.'

'I'm someone who's tendin' my own,' Burt answered. 'Name's Lane.'

Maber looked hard at Burt. 'If it turns out you're runnin' up a wrong color, mister, you can bet we'll meet again. Like Rush, I remember faces.'

'So where're you from, Lane?' Pruett, demanded this time.

'North,' Burt answered unhurriedly.

'That narrows it down some,' Herrick contributed with a sly smile. 'What do you make o' the local chaffer?'

'I was hopin' I'd rode away from a range war, not into one,' Burt replied with a similar, wily smile. 'I've been workin' for Noble Rockford up at the Musselshell.'

Maber took a long hard look at Burt, pointed his finger, with an implicit threat. Then, with the man called Rush, he walked from the saloon. They were followed closely by their well-armed colleagues into the street.

Grif Pruett grinned at Burt. 'I'd be *real* careful

where you tread, Lane,' he advised.

Burt held up a hand in concession to the marshal's well-intended warning. Then he walked over to the batwings and cast a wary eye along the street. 'Just seein' 'em safely out o' town,' he said, loud enough for the lawmen to hear.

'Weren't there some trouble up at Musselshell, a couple o' years back?' Pruett quietly asked Herrick.

'Yeah, they had 'emselves a sheep problem. An' from what I recall, it was Noble Rockford that was mixed up in it.'

'That's where Rush Pleasants must have recognized Lane from,' Pruett, deduced. 'An' maybe why that feller Maber weren't gettin' involved. I heard there was a lot more'n mutton got burned.'

Brax turned an interested eye on the two lawmen. 'Easy enough to check it out,' he said. 'It'd be funny, if they'd been chased across the border by that feller, only to run straight into him down here.'

'Yeah, real funny. But don't go makin' up a story just yet,' Herrick advised. 'I'll allow he's a man that looks like trouble. But somehow I don't think he's here to make it.'

Out in the street, the six sheepmen were on their way out of town. Taking point, Vaughn Maber nodded almost imperceptibly, threw a menacing glance at Burt, as he rode past.

From beneath the saloon's porch, Burt watched the riders kicking dust for a moment, before shrugging and turning away.

'Is my pa still in there?' a trimly dressed girl asked, as she suddenly appeared on the sidewalk beside him.

Burt raised a finger to the brim of his hat, looked into the girl's dark eyes. 'If he ain't rode in an' out with the sheepmen, I guess he might be,' he said, trying to get a general picture.

'No. He's Fraser Brax, owner of the *Tidings*.'

Burt thought for a moment. 'Oh him, yeah, I know who you mean,' he said. 'He's at the bar. I think he's discussin' the likelihood of a range war.'

'It's called selling newspapers,' the girl laughed. 'He's probably looking for a headline.'

'So, you want me to get him for you?' Burt asked.

The girl shook her head. 'No. No need,' she said, peering over the batwings. 'For the moment, he's safe enough.'

'Between two lawmen,' Burt acknowledged with a smile and tipped his hat once again.

2

Under the overhang of the Fallen Drummer, the owners of the Single Rig ranch stood side by side. Near them was Brewster Carron, the owner of Ankle Iron. It was the sheepmen leaving Lefty Detes who had caught their attention.

Jethro Poole twisted his right hand in the palm of his left. 'Could have had ourselves some fun there,' he said as they watched the riders leave town.

'Our time'll come soon enough,' his brother Jake suggested mischievously.

The men stood and speculated on what had happened in Lefty Detes, got more curious as people congregated on the sidewalk outside. As Warner Herrick walked towards them, Jethro muttered for Jake look up. Then they glanced at Brewster Carron, waited for the sheriff who was now accompanied by Grif Pruett.

'We'll accompany you boys back inside,' Herrick said with an encouraging grin, indicated that the cattlemen re-enter the saloon.

Through the mob of boisterous cowboys, the group pushed their way to the bar.

'I guess you must be waitin' for a scoop,' Herrick said, and called for a bottle of whiskey.

'Yeah, fit to bust,' Jethro answered. 'Them mutton punchers your new drinkin' companions, Sheriff?'

Herrick grinned. 'Did you see the feller who came out behind 'em? The one who stood watchin' 'em leave.'

'Yeah, I saw him,' Jake said. 'Who is he?'

The sheriff recalled the sheepmen's accusation that Burt Lane was in the pay of the cattlemen. 'Well, it was because of him they left, an' there was *six* of 'em,' he said. 'That's notable in my book. His name's Lane. Maybe you heard of 'im?'

The Pooles and Carron shook their heads.

'There was a mouthy one who accused Lane o' throwin' in with you lot. I think Vaughn Maber saved him from spendin' the rest of his life as a cripple,' Herrick continued.

For the next few minutes, the cattlemen listened to Pruett and Herrick's account of the goings on at Lefty Detes. Not completely trusting, Herrick attempted to connect them with Burt Lane, but he got nothing to confirm the sheepmens' suspicions.

When they heard of Fraser Brax's theory that someone had bought up Wild Meddow, Jethro Poole turned to Brewster Carron and expressed a thought.

'It ain't *you* who's secretly gone an' taken over that

13

land, is it?' he asked him.

Carron shook his head. 'No. I never figured I'd need more range,' he said. 'But there *was* a time though. A few years back when I was in Sheridan, I had a look into the records. The Meddow land could've been picked up for next to nothin' on owed taxes, but they'd been paid up.'

Jethro gave Carron a sharp look. 'You mean someone owns it? Who'd that be?'

'Yeah. I thought there was only three members o' the family,' Jake put in. 'Meddows that lived there, anyways.'

'Meddows that *died* there,' Carron corrected. 'There's three graves.'

Herrick drained his glass. 'That don't mean there's anythin' snaky gone on. Besides, I've made my thoughts clear about the chances o' cowmen sellin' out to sheepmen.'

'So what's what?' Jake asked.

'Like I been tellin' the doom merchants o' this town if anyone does move on to land that don't belong to 'em, me an' a big bad posse'll scuttle 'em back to where they came from,' the sheriff threatened.

Jethro took a step away from the bar. 'Obliged for the drink, Sheriff, but me an' Jake got a long ride back.'

'Yeah, me too,' Carron added.

'Keep your powder dry,' Pruett responded without further ado, as Herrick re-filled their glasses.

Outside of the saloon, Jake Poole followed his brother and Carron along to where their horses were hitched.

'What *was* that all about?' he asked, looking around, half hoping to spot a vulnerable sheepman.

'I think it was the law wantin' to know where we stood on the employ o' gun sharks,' Jethro said.

'Yeah,' Carron agreed, 'well, maybe we should start thinkin' about it. If any o' them sheepguts got a claim on the old Wild Meddow range, how are we goin' to keep 'em out? It sounds like they could be movin' real fast.'

'But they ain't there yet. Me an' Jake'll run our own cattle across the south fork, if we have to stop 'em. Just see if we don't,' Jethro warned.

'So who the hell's this Lane feller, who's got the sheriff quakin'?' Jake wondered, as Carron pondered a moment.

Jethro shrugged as they walked on. 'Maybe he's an opportunist . . . a pioneer salesman o' sheep dip. You say you ain't heard o' him?' Jethro queried of Carron.

'That's what I said, yeah. But I think I *have* . . . not too sure where or when, though. I'm wonderin' how Dodgson's man knew him. Unless they've *all* been meddlin' in stuff they shouldn't.'

'Why don't we find the man an' ask *him*?' Jake suggested. 'From what Herrick said happened at Lefty Detes, he ain't exactly in cahoots with 'em.'

Jethro nodded his approval. 'Yeah, OK. Tell the boys to ride back,' he said.

*

It didn't take long for the three of them to discover that Burt Lane wasn't in town.

'Do you reckon *you* can run some cattle on to Wild Meddow?' Jethro asked Carron, as they sat their horses, having checked at the livery. 'It could be you gets hurt first.'

'Ha, I don't reckon so. I'll put some grown stuff over as soon as I can. I ain't goin' to be left out o' this.'

'Then we'll see you down there,' Jethro promised.

'Good, but somethin' else strikes me,' Carron said. 'Them sheep up north o' the ridge? Well, it's a trick. There ain't enough of 'em. The big numbers are closer to Wild Meddow . . . much closer. They'll be spread munchin' along the foothills, an' we're goin' to have to stop 'em.'

'Oh yeah, sounds better than punchin' a herd o' cows. Maybe I'll get me that funnin' after all,' Jake enthused.

'I told you so,' Jethro said. 'But we'll stand off and use rifles. If Dodgson an' Maber are surrounded by paid gunnies, we don't want any of our boys hurt 'cause o' recklessness, do we?'

'No, we certainly don't want any o' that,' Jake agreed with a slight, puzzled look.

'An' another thought,' Carron said.

'What's it this time, Brew?'

'Maybe this Lane feller's been hired by Yearlin'

16

Timms. Maybe he's lookin' out for Red Ribbon.'

'It's a thought, but it ain't likely,' Jethro said. 'Timms wouldn't go it alone without tellin' one of us. But I would like to know what he's doin' here though,' he added thoughtfully as he wheeled his horse south for the Single Rig ranch.

3

Ten miles south of Clayburn, Burt rode into Elk Valley. East of the Needle Pikes, it was fertile Wyoming land that hugged the Montana margins. There was a far bigger settlement than he'd expected, but no more than his father had seen coming, many years before.

An hour after sundown, small squares of yellow light gave form to the distant homes. The county marshal was right, but Burt was still surprised to see farm buildings flanking the south bank of Gray Bull Creek. Skirting the Springfield Hogback, they extended eastward to the twin forks of the creek and the fringes of the Wild Meddow ranch, then on to the wooding stations of the Bighorn River.

The stars were bright and the moon was at full wax as Burt crossed the creek on to rangeland that hadn't shouldered cattle for many a year. The Wild Meddow was a big wedge of territory that was protected by natural boundaries. But only from men who recognized the rights of others. Cole Dodgson and Vaughn Maber weren't the first sheepmen to cast grabby eyes on that range and to try taking it.

Burt rode slowly in at the old ranch. During years of neglect, the roads and trails had overgrown with wild plants and grass, until they were totally buried. Store sheds had fallen apart, and posted corrals had perished, rotted into the ground. The long house facing the creek was built wholly of stone, but its roof had collapsed and all windows and doors were gone.

In waist-high lupins that fronted the barn, Burt hauled in his mare. For a minute or so he levelled his gaze towards the home side of the creek's north fork. He knew that on rising ground, and beneath a grove of blue beech, there were three headstones. They were the graves of the Meddow family who'd been shot dead by the sheepmen.

There was no change in Burt's steely expression. He'd got work to do, wasn't going to dwell on a cheerless past. He reasoned that as soon as Dodgson and Maber got themselves moved out of Clayburn, they'd be riding on to Wild Meddow land. He moved slowly around the old barn, then he turned east, rode to the foot of the Springfield Hogback.

Burt headed for an old track that began a mile beyond the ranch, though now it was no more than a scar over the high wall up which it led. But, despite the years since he'd last rode it, he knew the trail well. He eased the roan through the shallow scree, and then for a half hour more climbed steadily to the low timber that capped the sharp-rising slope. In a fissure, he found the cover he was seeking and drew in to unpack and rest. With his back against a gnarled and stunted pine, he ate pie crust, sweet onions and a corn dodger, washed it down with a mouthful of tepid canteen water.

A short while later, Burt walked to the rim of the ridge, gazed out into the blue-black shadows of the ranch land. The scent of sweet clover drifted up, but nothing pierced the night except the flicker of a dying fire.

As he looked down on what was meant to be a hideaway camp, Burt spat contemptuously. They were sheepmen far below him, and they'd already staked out the western approach to the Wild Meddow. His gut tightened as he realized the sheepmen had been ready to move the day that he'd rode into Clayburn.

The far, north side of the creek fork was choked with virgin timber. Beneath the western escarpment where he now stood, open clearings were dashed with sandy benches that had collapsed from the wall of the ridge. Around them, cloaked by a growth of low thicket were scattered the weathered bones of sheep. Burt couldn't see them, but he knew they were there – the dumb animals that had attempted to overrun the Wild Meddow. Most of them had been killed with rifle fire, but many of them had formed a terrified gather, and suffocated to death.

There was no evidence yet of sheep breaching

either the north or south forks of Gray Bull Creek, and Burt backed off from the rim. Depending on how near the incoming flocks were, and if the men who already occupied the western end of the Wild Meddow got help in time, he thought it was possible to keep them out single-handed.

Back at the gnarled pine, Burt pulled off his boots and rolled himself into his blanket, then his slicker. Succumbing to the dull pain from his bodily and mental tiredness, he fell almost immediately into sleep. It had been a long day, but he woke soon after two o'clock. It was near enough to the hour he'd selected as his eyes had closed.

In the early cold, he ate more jerk and another dodger. He considered kindling a small fire to make coffee, but decided to do without. He saddled the roan, started the walk back down the ridge.

Burt led his horse around the foot of the ridge. He avoided the shrubs and weeds until he got closer to where the sheepmen's camp was hidden. There were still no sounds, but although the moon was now down, the stars gave him some visibility. He slipped the bridle for the horse to graze and lifted the .45 carbine from its saddle-boot.

Out over the Bighorns, the eastern horizon was just starting to lighten up, and Burt advanced warily. Three saddle horses and a pack horse were hobbled in a clearing that was surrounded by dense brushwood. The animals lifted their heads and smelled him, then returned to their graze. Quietly,

Burt went around the clearing, until the gleaming ripples of Gray Bull Creek appeared beyond. The camp was set against the south bank, the Wild Meddow side. Near to their riding gear, three men were asleep, and snoring noisy.

Burt weighed up the situation, grinned to himself and backtracked to the horses in the clearing. In a few minutes he'd removed the hobbles, tossed them into the darkness and walked the horses towards the foot of the ridge. He knew that if the horses continued north, they'd end up running straight back to their home ground. He guessed that wouldn't be too far from Clayburn.

Burt watched the pale blue light spread slowly across the Wyoming sky. Having sent the horses packing, he could now do the same to the sheepmen. If he wasn't going to kill them, he'd have to come up with a good threat, tender an ominous future. He hunkered between two low-spread willows, pulled the brim of his hat down, and decided to wait, consider his predicament.

A little over an hour later, and Burt's eyes were shaded from the rising sun. He sniffed at the drifting smoke, heard the noises raised by the sheepmen as they busied themselves around their fire. A man carrying feed bags passed close by, and Burt sucked in his breath, waited for him to return.

A moment later, the expected shout came from the clearing. The man came running back, dashed straight to his camp which was ahead and to the right of where Burt was hiding. 'Get up, all o' you, the stock's took off,' he yelled.

Another voice opened with an exasperated curse. 'They're hobbled down, Pugg. They ain't goin' far. Now's chow time.'

Tin plates were already clattering when Burt thumbed a cartridge into the breech of his carbine. He walked quietly to within twenty feet of their breakfast fire.

'Those hobbled-down horses are south o' the creek by now,' he called out and levered the trigger guard for effect. 'Gives you lamb lickers a real problem.'

The three men rocked forward on to their knees, but didn't turn around.

'Stand up, an' drop your gunbelts,' Burt went on. 'Step away, an' keep lookin' east.'

Wordless, the three followed Burt's orders and moved to one side of the fire. Burt stepped up behind them, scooped up the holstered Colts and cartridge belts and tossed them over to where he'd been standing. 'Now, let's get ourselves introduced,' he said, levelling the rifle as the men turned to face him.

'It's the cowpoke from town,' Pleasants rasped, after a short moment. 'He's the one I been tellin' you about.'

The dirt-grimed faces of the other two men studied Burt with uneasy curiosity.

'You got a problem with us, mister?' one of them

23

asked, uncertain of Burt's support.

'Yeah, you're a mile or two off your bedground.' There was clear forewarning in Burt's response.

'This here's goin' to be sheep country. An' *that* kind o' gives us lawful rights.'

Burt's jaw twitched uneasily again. 'There's a pile o' bones close by that gives true meanin' to them "lawful rights",' he said scornfully. 'Are you men workin' for Maber or Dodgson?'

'Both. What's the difference?'

'Maybe it's the way you got o' stayin' alive.'

'An' now I've remembered who you are,' Rush Pleasants said apprehensively. 'Are you thinkin' o' doin' to us what you did to them boys up along the Musselshell?'

Burt eyed the man circumspectly, shifted the gun's muzzle a little higher. 'They had their chances, but preferred to die,' he rasped. '*You* get to jump stubble. So, if you all want to move out o' here, get your boots off.'

'I ain't takin' nothin' off, an' I ain't walkin' nowhere, either.' Pleasants declared.

Burt's finger moved very slightly on the trigger, but the explosion was sudden and violent, made him blink. 'Can't trust goddamn short-barreled firearms,' he muttered, grinned malevolently, as the bullet ripped up through the brim of one of the other men's hats.

'You think you might regret not shootin' us, mister,' the man said, grinding his teeth, starting to

24

drag at one of his boots.

'If I'm still around when you make it out o' this place, it'll be *you* regrettin' it, take my word,' Burt countered. 'Get some more wood on to the fire.'

Burt waited until the skewered meats were black and charred remains, then he kicked the men's boots in among them. He made them strip down to their grimy underclothes, toss their cloths into the fire until the flames pranced and crackled high. With his carbine in one hand, and his Colt in the other, he walked the cursing bunch back along the creekside to the foot of the Springfield Hogback.

'Go find your stinkin' sheep, an' run south with 'em. If I even get to smellin' you again, I promise you'll get more'n foot blisters.' There was no doubt that Burt's warning was sincere and unconditional.

He watched them move off, headed for their punishing walk across the rangeland. The heat would increase during the day, become crippling as the sun climbed. 'That's good,' Burt said to himself, and made his way back to their camp.

He retrieved the gunbelts from where he'd thrown them. They were plain, contained cheaply made .36 Colts and he tossed them into the surging flames. He grimaced as the cartridges began to explode, but he was already hurrying to his grazing roan.

Burt pushed the rifle back into its boot, then started back up the narrow file to his hideout perch, high on the ridge.

An hour later, and returned to his gnarled pine,

he stared unhappily at the remnants of his meagre victuals. He was safe for a while though, and decided on a fire and hot coffee. He knew that trackers would eventually come, that within an hour of Rush Pleasants and his partners setting out barefoot, his threats wouldn't amount to a hill of beans. They'd return with a small army, but before realizing he'd taken to higher ground, they'd start looking for him in the upper end of the valley. Eventually they'd discover his trail from the base of the ridge, and sometime during the day, he'd have to find some other vantage point. So, he'd rest up until mid-morning, then take a look out from the rim.

4

No one showed until an hour before noon. Burt was expecting some action from beyond the ridge, so was surprised by a bunch of riders approaching Wild Meddow land from the north. Carried by the breeze, he heard the soft clink of tack over the dull pounding of hoofs. The men rode tight, and Burt guessed they were from Ankle Iron, that it would be the rancher, Brewster Carron, heading them up.

They followed the creek, turned east below Burt and made for the camp. There was no smoke now, but the tang of burned boot leather drifted low through the brush. The men drew rein, and within fifteen minutes, four of them were following the tracks of the sheepmen's hired guns. They went south, where they should, and where Burt expected them to, beyond the ridge into the rise of the Needle Pikes. The others made a resting site beneath a willow brake along the north fork of the creek.

Burt stared out across the scope of Wild Meddow's

range, remembered the Clayburn newspaperman's words about the dangerous and unstable gather of cattlemen and sheepmen.

The second group of horsemen didn't come unexpectedly. Burt saw them through the creek timber, and long before he caught their sound. He counted ten, and they were being led by Jake and Jethro Poole. They followed the trail of the Ankle Iron cowboys until they met at the temporary camp. Without a doubt, there was more in the offing than a cattlemen's association meeting, and a thin, disturbing smile cracked Burt's face.

It was late afternoon when the Ankle Iron riders returned from their trailing Rush Pleasants south from the Springfield Hogback. Burt had a few moments of concern, wondered if they'd start over and find his rising track. But after they'd done some talking, the combined force headed out fast and resolute through the south-western end of Wild Meddow.

'So you found some sheepmen,' Burt muttered in confirmation. He turned from the rim, struck his modest camp and saddled the roan.

Warily, he rode the ridge trail back to the valley floor, hugged the slopes before rising again into the foothills of the Pikes. He spotted no other rider as he continued further south, climbing higher into dense timber. He rode on to a spur of projecting rock, could still see no sign of the cattlemen's force below him.

Taking slanted paths through the aspen and pine, he moved off again. He figured the riders were close to the edge of the Pikes, but they were still moving south of the valley. He walked the roan, checked frequently for any sign of distant movement.

The sun was falling into the western horizon, nudging the far off Rockies, when the crackle of gunfire split the heavy silence of the range. From the edge of the timberline far below him, disturbed scrub jays took to the air, and Burt hauled in the roan.

The opening shots quickly rolled into a crescendo. A relentless pattern of gunfire crackled for ten minutes before the first let-up. Even then, the noise didn't cease completely. It faltered, trailed off further to the south around the curve of the slopes.

'Huh, they found somethin',' Burt said to his horse and rubbed its forehead. He kicked his heels, moved the roan quicker through the trees. He wanted to get further along the timberline, find a vantage point where he could see what was happening.

It was the sheepmen he saw first. They were holed up, spread along a rocky spine that broke from the Pikes. They were desperately fending off the cowmen, trying to stop them from getting to their stock.

But the attack was now double spearheaded. One small group of sheepmen had already been hit as they'd held up their panicky animals. Another group was taking cover behind one of their camp wagons, returning fire at the advancing cattlemen. Beyond them, further east into the range, herders were trying to string some sheep up towards the lower creek. It held a shallow crossing that would take them on to Wild Meddow land. Two sheepmen were making their way back towards the ridge. They had escaped the fire of the cowmen, were on foot, clambering through the tumble of rock and scree.

Burt continued his watch, noticed the sheep kills. They were laying half a mile from the shelter of the rocky spine, piled in small heaps where they'd bunched in their panic. It was where the fighting had started, where Brewster Carron and the Poole brothers had met up with the sheepmen.

Most of the killing had been dealt with by rifles at long range. But now the attacking force was closing in, using pistols as they circled the rocky spine.

Burt could see the sheepmen grabbing their horses. They were beginning a retreat into the brush between their scant cover and the start of the Pikes timberline.

Hidden from all but a lone, high-circling vulture, Burt looked down on the rout. 'I'll lay good money no sheepman ever led a military charge,' he muttered scornfully.

The sheepmen were terrified and disorganized in their flight, overwhelmed as the cattlemen's fire cut them down. More than five score of sheep escaped a fearsome death, but many more were left abandoned.

The gnaw of cordite whisped its way high into the foothills and it caused the roan to whicker. 'Easy, girl. Best a whiff o' smoke in this world than in another one,' Burt said, quiet and calmly.

The sheepmen were now out to save themselves as first dark arrived. There was no more gunfire as they scattered. For a half hour, there was hardly any sound, then Burt heard the crackle of burning wood. Two wagons had been set ablaze, with tongues of bright flame rising to the darkening sky. Then he saw the fast moving, small shadowy figures, heard the resurgence of rapid gunfire.

It was the cowmen killing the sheep. They were shooting then as fast as they could, would continue until they ran out of ammunition. Any remaining animals would hurtle unthinkingly for the stronghold of the Pikes or the open range beyond the settlements. It would be many days before the herders gathered them in, if ever.

Burt stared into the night sky, then closed his eyes for a moment. He let the memories of Musselshell return, his last involvement with sheepmen. Once, he'd done what the cowmen far below him were doing now, had had to. The destruction of any livestock didn't sit well with him, but he knew it was the only way. Dodgson and Maber would use their sheep as an invasion force, an assault weapon to munch and grind its way across the entire Elk Valley.

Whatever was happening on the range below him, Burt knew the sheepmen would return more

31

overbearing, more forceful. He felt the icy run of sweat between his shoulder blades and shivered, knew there'd be a lot more death before a lasting peace settled on cattle country.

5

Long after the last gun's echo cracked out, and the wagons were no more than charred embers, Burt contemplated his prospects. It was well into full dark now, no need for any more hiding. He climbed on to the roan, and for an hour he backtracked north.

Within sight of the Springfield Hogback he made himself a camp and some scalding coffee. In the early hours, and wearing an ironic smile, he fell asleep. He was head-counting the stock that would soon be coming down from Musselshell.

At sun up, he cooked the last of his provisions. It was a mixed skillet feast of salt pork strips, a can of Californian tomatoes and crumbled pone. He took his time packing, was looking out to where he was headed. It was north to the ridge, then west through the settlements, on to the Ankle Iron and across the creek to Wild Meddow.

Tugging at the horn of his saddle, he saw the distant trail line of slow-moving cattle. He held his

33

hat against the high arcing sun, squinted to make out detail.

'This can't be *them*. Not from Musselshell,' he muttered. 'Must be an Ankle Iron drive, on the way to new grass.' He had a last quick glance, then mounted up, took the trail to Wild Meddow.

Hours later, the roan trampled the thick corn-rose outside of the ranch's derelict buildings. Burt decided to make provisional use of the largest of the stone-walled sheds. He freed his bedroll and traps, unsaddled and set about moving fallen roof timbers. Later, when supplies could be freighted out from Clayburn, he'd do some work on the house and the barn. At noon, he had more thoughts of the Ankle Iron, wondered why they should be moving cattle. He speculated on the possibility of Brewster Carron fording the creek, came to the conclusion that he'd have to ride out and take a look.

Burt re-saddled the roan and set off at a dogged canter. He rode the willow brakes for an hour until he found the crossing point he was looking for, then the boulder-rimmed scrape that gave him the cover.

Well hidden, he sat his saddle, stared across the bright, shallow water into the range. He saw the big herd when they were less than a mile away. His thoughts were a good fit, and he saw the Ankle Iron cattle headed straight for Wild Meddow range.

Two men were riding point, but loose herders showed along the flanks of moving cattle. Burt didn't ride out to meet them, he waited patiently while they came towards him. The lead steer was less than a hundred yards off when he quit cover, splashed across the creek.

The two riders drew rein, were taken aback when Burt lifted a warning hand.

'I hope you boys ain't headed this way,' Burt drawled. 'It ain't the poor beeves who'll be payin' for trespass.'

'Trespass? What are you talkin' about? There ain't nobody here.'

Burt moved a hand to the butt of his Colt. '*I'm* here,' he warned.

One of riders was about to respond to Burt's confrontation, when two more riders came galloping up from the herd. One of them was Brewster Carron.

'What's the hold up?' he asked. 'Who the hell are *you?*' when he realized that Burt wasn't one of his own men. The man's features were haggard, worn tired. He scrutinized Burt, remembered the story of a man who'd run up against sheepmen in Clayburn.

Burt gestured at the cattle. 'Looks like your boys were set to stroll 'em on to my land. I sure wouldn't take too kindly to that.'

'*Your* land?' Carron queried, his interest turning suddenly to unease.

'Yeah, mine. *That's* your answer for the hold up.'

Carron's face broke in to a weary grin. 'So, you'll be Burt Lane, the man who burned down them fellers' camp an' set 'em afoot half naked?'

No emotion stirred in Burt's face as he nodded his

head. 'Sheepmen got no business in this part o' the valley, or their hired guns. From what I saw last night, I reckon I ain't the only one who thinks that.'

Carron thought for a moment before saying anything. 'I heard you was a top waddy, up near the border,' he suggested.

'I worked for Noble Rockford, if that's what you mean, Mr Carron.'

The Ankle Iron boss held back a smile. 'You don't any more?'

'Nope. I'm here as a one-man-band. I'm bringin' in my own herd.'

Carron stared, let the smile develop. 'Well, kick my butt,' he exclaimed in slow surprise.

'First time I see one o' your beeves on my land, I might do just that,' Burt warned.

'Ha. You ain't playin' some goddamn trick, are you, Lane? Holdin' us up, so's the sheepmen can take over? You already seen what happened to Dodgson an' Maber.'

'No trick, Mr Carron, an' as yet it ain't personal. But as long as I'm able to pull a trigger, woollies ain't ever goin' to run on Wild Meddow land,' Burt levelled back at Carron.

Carron recognized Burt's uncompromising stance. From what he'd heard, what he could see, it was obvious the man facing him wasn't a natural or representative shepherd. He turned to his riders.

'Let the beef spread boys,' he ordered. 'There's enough green on this side o' the creek to please 'em.'

Carron's riders had a look behind them, decided to hang around for a minute or two.

'You say you're runnin' an outfit up here on your own?' Carron asked.

Burt nodded. 'Yeah. But I ain't talkin' your size bunch. With the natural boundaries o' Wild Meddow helpin' me, one man can handle the numbers I got in mind.'

For a moment, Carron considered what Burt had got planned. 'Then you sleep while there's a whole moon,' he advised. 'You don't want any irate sheepman sneakin' up on you with them big cutters.'

'Yeah, well I guess they'll be tryin'. Like *you* were, up until ten minutes ago.'

'We had good reason,' Carron replied. 'We wanted some sort o' bulwark to protect ourselves against the sheep. They don't call 'em hoof locusts for nothin'. You said yourself, there's natural boundaries out o' the Hogback.'

'Who's the *we* you're talkin' about?' Burt asked.

'The Poole brothers. Jake an' Jethro. They're trailin' a herd that ought to be this way sometime tomorrow.'

'I'd hate to see 'em go to all that trouble,' Burt said calmly. 'I'd appreciate you sendin' word for 'em to disperse or turn around. From now on, what goes for sheep, goes for any other man's beef.'

Carron nodded his understanding. 'That's plain enough,' he replied. Face-to-face, he was inclined towards Burt's sincerity, his obvious intent. Twisting around in the saddle, he spoke to one of his men. 'Pitt, ride back an' tell Jake an' Jethro to hold up. Don't explain nothin'. Just tell 'em I said to.'

The cowboy nodded once, turned his horse south and kicked his spurs.

'Much obliged. Now, I got me some repairs an' renovations to take care of,' Burt said to Carron. He nudged the roan, walked it to the creek crossing, the way back on to his land. Carron watched until Burt had made it to the far side of the creek. 'I wonder how long he is in *this* town?' he muttered.

6

In the days that followed, Clayburn was shaken by stories of the battle between the sheepmen and cattlemen. Hundreds of sheep had been trapped, run down and shot dead. Many men had been killed or badly wounded during the long, drawn-out fight. That was the gathering news. Reports that were added to daily, as cowboys left piecemeal information in the town's bars, beaneries and boarding houses.

According to the stories, there was little doubt that the cowmen had made an offensive in order to protect themselves. No sheepmen had been seen in town, but again, it was rumoured that Dodgson and Maber were seen in Clover City. They'd been busy with lawyers, making demands for a lawful safeguard.

It was publication day of the *Clayburn Tidings* when the news first broke in town. For two days, Fraser

Brax sought to establish facts from the rumours. For a special edition of his newspaper, he tried to further dramatize events by placing the fight on Wild Meddow land. But considering the parties involved, he thought better of it. Due to the lack of other articles, he actually had next to nothing for the regular issue, couldn't make up more than a single broadsheet.

Late one morning, frustrated by the situation, he left his copy desk. He called out to his daughter who was sorting advertisements in the print room.

'Hester, I'm goin' to try an' run down these rumours. There's got to be truthful copy, somewhere out there.'

Hester's dark eyes sparkled. 'That's what a quality newspaperman would do, Pa,' she said affectionately. 'Call in at the marshal's office, why don't you? That's always a font of reliable information.'

Brax turned and smiled, wagged a finger at Hester's humour. Within ten minutes, he was sipping whiskey at Lefty Detes with Grif Pruett. He expressed his concern about the lack of a dependable witness.

Pruett listened politely, then shook his head. 'Well, I don't know any more than you,' he said. 'Less than that, maybe. Along this street, there's as many different stories as there are piles o' horse dung. I tend to step round 'em.'

'I got my newshounds in the Fallen Drummer, an' there's no word about what really happened. You'd think the bear's bile *they* sell would loosen up any cowboy's tongue,' Brax said.

'Not if they want to draw pay at the end of the month,' Pruett ventured. 'Don't you think the likes o' Brew Carron would o' threatened 'em with what would happen if anyone blabbed?'

'I'm sure he has. But I usually get a snippet. It's not always the most accurate, an' not always *news*, but it's copy.'

Pruett puffed his dissent. 'Well, not this time, Fraser,' he said. 'An' don't forget, they'll be on fightin' wages. Besides, if you print the truth, it'll read like an unprovoked attack. We got laws against that sort o' thing. Even big-time cowmen know that.'

While Brax stared mystified into the back bar, Yearling Timms and the Poole brothers pushed their way through the batwings. It was a twist of fate that Timms's head appeared too big for his body, and that his eyes bulged big.

The cowmen acknowledged Brax and Pruett as they made for the bar. A fresh bottle of whiskey was produced, and more drinks were poured all round.

'Anythin' in what we been hearin' about a big gunfight below the Pikes?' Brax pursued his enquiries.

Jethro Poole gave a dry smile. 'We've all been hearin' a lot o' wild yarns,' he answered. 'I can understand your interest, Fraser, what with bein' a newspaperman an' all. But so far none of us have seen any evidence.'

41

'What evidence would *that* be of then?' Brax asked hopefully.

'All the dead an' wounded. You'd think there'd be remains o' battle ... somethin' to show for a big gunfight.'

Brax detected a slight, twisted grin on Jake Poole's mouth, and Timms was holding a snigger. The newsman didn't know of any wounded men who'd been brought into town, and he'd checked that the doctor hadn't made a recent call to any of the ranches. Likewise, he knew the undertaker hadn't dug any holes.

Brax's frustration welled up still more when Burt Lane made his way into the saloon. He was suddenly suspicious that the man who'd appeared to be a drifter was somehow involved with the cattlemen. He watched, smiled at the meaning of cowboys picking up sign.

But that wasn't to be. Burt Lane didn't order a drink. He approached the cowmen and settled his gaze on the owner of the Red Ribbon ranch.

'You'll be Yearlin' Timms?' he asked, but it sounded like he already knew the answer.

The green calf-featured man looked steadily back at Burt. 'Somethin' I can do for you?'

'Yep. I've got five hundred head o' she-stuff closin' on your western range. If the boys drivin' the herd have made any kind o' time, we're talkin' sundown. So, I'd like your OK to cross the Red Ribbon. It'll be just north o' the Bull Creek.'

Timms shrugged. 'There's a mile-wide stock lane, that side o' the water,' he said. 'You don't need my permission.'

Burt nodded briefly. 'I knew it. I was just makin' sure *you* did,' he retorted.

'So what we heard's right, is it?' Jethro Poole enquired. 'You're goin' into the cow business.'

'I'm already in the cow business,' Burt answered.

'Your own cattle?'

'O' course they're my own. They might've carried the Rockford's mark once upon a time.'

'You sure them ranches up along the Musselshell ain't migratin' south?'

A thin smile moved fleetingly across Burt's face. 'That sounds like a civil way o' sayin' somethin' else,' he suggested. 'If it's any o' your business, I got all them cows the hard way. Most of 'em was wages from Rockford.'

'Yeah, that sounds right, Jethro,' Jake Poole spoke up. 'They're slashed-vent branded. There's two an' three year olds. Some's recent.'

Jethro grinned cordially at Burt. 'Well, there you go, young feller,' he said. 'We all wish you the luck you're goin' to need.'

Burt nodded. 'So, how'd you know about the brands on my cattle?' he asked, turning enquiringly to Jethro's brother.

'Some trail hands I took on said they saw 'em. Three men, drivin' upwards o' four hundred head. They're north west o' town, slantin' towards the creek.'

'Hmm, sounds like I already got some o' that luck I'm needin',' Burt said. 'They've made good time. Reckon I'll go help bring 'em in.'

7

'Lane's got himself a fair-sized parcel o' land, sure enough, but there's too few cows, an' even fewer pokes,' Jethro Poole's said. 'We need an outfit three or four times the size he's aimin' to run.'

'He won't last long,' Timms added. 'Not *above* the ground he won't.'

Marshal Pruett eyed the men with some distaste. 'Burt Lane weren't part o' that fight. He saw what happened, but he weren't part of it,' he stated.

'Those goddamn maggot men don't know that,' Timms scoffed.

'Did you fellers pass the mercantile on the way in?' Pruett asked.

'Yeah, we rode past. Why?' Jethro asked back.

'You'd have seen Pinch Cutler's bull train. They was loadin' with an interestin' heap o' stuff. Him an' a couple o' packers. There was everythin' from sawed timber to flour.'

'What are you sayin', Marshal?' Jethro wanted to

45

know, after short consideration.

'I'm sayin' that Lane's bought all that stuff, an' he's hired Pinch to haul it out to Wild Meddow. It don't look much like he's thinkin' o' movin' on.'

'Do you figure he's strong enough to stand up to the sheepmen?' Fraser Brax wondered. The cowmen regarded Brax amusedly for a moment, and Yearling Timms coughed up a short laugh.

'Laugh all you want,' Brax said. 'But like you, Lane's a cowman. If he goes under, before long it'll be settlement land, an' sheep really don't know the difference.'

'Maybe, but it ain't happened yet,' Jethro rumbled, and called for another bottle.

On the way out of town, Burt saw the last of his goods being lifted from the loading platform. There were three ox wagons already full, and canvas covers were being tied down. Burt estimated his cattle would be arriving on Wild Meddow about the same time.

He left Clayburn and rode north along the border road, stayed on it until he saw where the herd would swing east to the stock lane and Gray Bull Creek. He lifted the roan to a gallop, and before mid day found the herd nooning among timber to the east of the Needle Pikes.

The three drovers had a pack train of eight extra horses that also belonged to Burt. Two of the men were unknown to him, but the third raised himself from where he'd been resting and extended his hand in greeting.

'Hey, Burt,' he hollered. 'Looks like all of us made it.'

'Yeah, we all made it, Milo, an' you in real good time,' Burt said, shaking hands and smiling broadly.

As Milo Tedder led Burt over to the young cowboys he'd brought with him, he said the ride had gone well. He made the introductions, told Burt about Noble Rockford's message. 'Said I was to tell you your job's still open if you want to come back to it.'

'Yeah, I know that. But this is somethin' I've spent my growin' years thinkin' on,' Burt told him.

'Yeah. One o' them things that's got to be done,' Tedder understood. 'Mr Rockford reckoned you'd still be of that mind. He said that he's always got cattle you can make a deal on, an' he's thrown in twenty head o' range bulls for goodwill.'

Soon afterwards they moved the cattle out, strung them south to the stock lane. Burt rode alongside his old friend, continuously admired the quality of the shorthorns.

They made one more night camp on the trail, then next afternoon crossed the north fork of Gray Bull Creek on to Wild Meddow land. Burt pushed them all on to where the north and south forks met, turned them loose within sight of the ranch house.

'Just so's they'll know where home is,' he told the Rockford cowboys. 'Then they can drift where they please.'

The Rockford men were surprised that Wild Meddow ranch had been so abandoned. Tedder had a good look over the place, recognized its value. He recalled Rockford saying that when Burt had took off south, he was more than likely heading for a two-by-four outfit, maybe taking up an open range claim. But Tedder could see that that wasn't so. He knew that Burt had put all of his earned dollars into the small, quality herd. There was some big work ahead, but he could see it was a worthwhile venture.

Pinch Cutler's bull train pulled in at sundown that night. For a safer crossing, the tough old bullwhacker had taken the train further down the creek to where it shallowed, crossed within a mile of the home pasture.

At sun-up the following morning, the cowboys helped the packers start to unload the big wagons. Building materials were stacked between the barn and the dilapidated sheds, some simple furniture and a cooking stove were carried straight into the house.

Late in the afternoon, when Cutler's outfit was gone, Tedder decided they'd stay over. Noble Rockford hadn't set them a particular time for getting back, so they'd rest up a while before returning to Musselshell.

'We could help out, Burt,' Tedder offered. 'Make the roof sound . . . watertight at least.'

The men did more than that. First, they set up the Dutch oven, enabling them to cook food and stay on a while longer. They cleared the sheds and patched the barn, burned off the rotted corral posts and set new ones. The cattle moved slowly to the east, spread themselves between the containment boundaries of the creeks.

Of the five rooms in the house, Burt managed to fix up three of them. The immediate ground, in and around the buildings, was also cleared and turned.

'Maybe I'll get a couple o' goats to keep the weeds down. I hear tell them an' sheep are real close relatives.'

The cowboys sniggered. 'Heh heh, have 'emselves a war dance,' Tedder chuckled.

Soon, the ranch began to take on the appearance of a working outfit, of someone living and working there. The night before the Rockford cowboys were to leave, Tedder glanced thoughtfully at Burt.

'I rode up to them willows at the creek today,' he said. 'Looks like there's a whole family buried there. Their name was Meddow. I guess it was them that built this place.'

Burt nodded his head. 'Yeah I guess it was. An' now, *I'm* here,' he said, quiet and unrevealing.

'Well, it's a fine spread,' Tedder declared. 'There's good water, an' timber along the north fork an' plenty o' rich grass. Looks like you got the done well trappin's, eh Burt?'

Stay around a while longer and you might not be thinking that, Burt thought. He thanked the men for staying on, for their work. He didn't mention the battle that had already taken place in the sheep and cattle war, and didn't ask if they were passing through Clayburn on the way home.

That was what Milo Tedder and his two young companions did though. It was at the noisy, crowded bar of the Fallen Drummer that they heard murmurings of the range war. They decided to split up and learn more, meet at Lefty Detes to consider their findings.

The men from Musselshell were surprised at what was happening in the valley, what had already happened out below the Needle Pikes. On Burt Lane's part, Tedder worried that Wild Meddow lay wide open to sudden onslaught. He knew the likely outcome, because something like it had happened once before.

'I'm sorry, boys, but there's no time for cuttin' any wolves loose. My old partner Burt's at the heart o' real trouble,' he told his men. 'We'll get on home, an' if Mr Rockford still wants to be of any help, I'm thinkin' there is a way.'

8

Burt knew full well he wasn't a long way from trouble, knew he'd have to give serious thought to the dangers of Wild Meddow. He wouldn't leave though, not now he'd got the ranch house patched and some homely comforts. In its defence against sheepmen, he'd remain on his land for as long as possible. He'd get some geese for the yard. They were first-rate guards and protectors, gave raucous alarm of any approach. He thought maybe one of the settlement farms could supply him with a grouchy bird or two when he went to buy stock feed.

One early morning, not long after the Noble Rockford men had departed, he walked the roan through the willow brakes, across the south fork of Gray Bull Creek. As far as he could see, homesteads were spreading to the east. They were mainly squared-off plots of corn, but there was some beet and vegetables, even fruit trees. More distant fields were dotted with seed-raiding crows.

Most of the houses were smartly painted. Work buildings were in good order, turkey fences were neat and tight. At the first farm, he inquired of a man who was stripping peas from a garden plot.

'Try the Barrows,' the man said unenthusiastically. 'Keep to the creek, an' they're next along. You can get grain from 'em. They've got enough.'

The Barrow people were the first to journey west of the Bighorns, far into the valley. The entire family worked in the fields to take their share of the ploughing and planting. Ruse Barrow was a plump, good-natured man who left his cold-blood mare when he saw Burt approaching. Burt introduced himself, said he was in the market for cereal to feed his saddle-brokes.

The man smeared some dirt away from his nose and mouth. Thinking for a moment before responding, he took off his slouch hat and replaced it. 'You livin' up there?' he asked, inclined his head in the direction of Wild Meddow.

'I do. Got nearly as much land as you,' Burt said and smiled.

Barrow's shrewd eyes didn't move much, but Burt knew the man had done a fair estimation of him. He wondered if he was likely to pay something weighty for the grain.

Barrow smiled back. 'Well, I got plenty o' what you need,' he said. 'It's just a quirk of fate I guess that what us poor farmers breakfast on, you big augars feed to your stock.'

Burt grimaced at the soft mocking, shook his head. 'What I get to breakfast on's usually to do with what I earn,' he chided. 'An' I ain't a big augar . . . not yet. Sounds like you got other ranchers buyin' from you?' he followed up with.

'No, they don't . . . won't buy from *us*. They reckon that if they create a well-located market, there'll be even more settlers,' the man said regretfully. 'They're content to buy from Clayburn or Clover City at twice the price they'd be payin' us. So, bearin' that in mind, if you let me an' my boys haul your feed grain, I'll charge you ten dollars a load. That's about fifty sacks.'

'That sounds like a fair deal,' Burt said, pondering the remains of his stake.

Barrow told him to ride around to the barn where he'd meet him. The man's wife and two grown daughters who were scything hogweed close to the barn smiled shyly when Burt rode up. There were some heavily jowelled dogs running around and Burt watched them, interested in their tetchy play.

A minute or two later Barrow appeared. He shouted a terse command at the dogs, and indicated for Burt to dismount. He showed Burt the granary, the quality of what he was growing, and Burt was more than satisfied.

'Spiky dogs,' he said, but Barrow was more interested in making a deal on the feed.

'OK, I'll take a hundred sacks. Fifty of oats an' fifty o' barley, with a ten per cent discount for cash,' Burt offered, and was already counting out the bills.

The two men shook hands, and Barrow, pointed to a smoke house, midway between the barn and the creek. Burt could hear the sound of snuffles and yips as they got close, then a low, defensive snarl when Barrow drew the door bolt.

A dog bared its fangs, braced itself a few feet away from the inside of the door. Over Barrow's shoulder, Burt peered in and discovered why. Beyond the dog was a bitch. In the far corner was a pair of plump, heaving pups with identical markings.

'Jeez, they're the size o' bear cubs,' Burt exclaimed and backed off a step.

Barrow spoke a soothing word and closed the door very gently. 'Well, they're sure as ornery. They're American Bulldogs, an' I got to keep 'em in there a spell,' he said. 'You don't want 'em near anythin' smaller'n a bab moose at whelp time.'

Burt looked suitably impressed. 'American, eh? That's very partisan of you, Mr Barrow. Do they make for guard dogs?' he asked.

'Yeah, an' they don't ever back off, not when they got their teeth into somethin',' Barrow laughed calculatingly. 'You *can* school 'em, an' generally they're a one-man, one-family dog,' he added proudly.

'Taters an' peas need that sort o' defendin', do they?' Burt said with a dry smile.

Barrow returned the smile. 'Wife's from border country. Her family have bred 'em for a couple o' generations, apparently. Over the years, they've sort o' grown on *me*. Like I said, they're faithful, an' that's more'n can be said o' some folk.'

'Do you want to sell 'em . . . the pups?' Burt asked.

Barrow shrugged. 'No, but what can I do?' he said sadly. 'Hand me another twenty, an' they'll be on the load tomorrow. In a few months time, there'll be nobody but nobody crossin' them creeks.'

While they discussed the dogs and their feeding routine, Burt wondered if the sheepmen would be recognizing those 'few months'. He was thinking that two fully grown bulldogs was a clear improvement on geese, but he saw that Ruse Barrow's mind had moved on to something else.

There was a moment of silence before the farmer spoke. 'Outside o' the mercantile, we heard the sheep an' cattle outfits had a bit of a battle,' he said.

'Just as well you weren't standin' outside o' the Fallen Drummer,' Burt replied. 'That would o' probably stretched it to an all out war.'

'Well, we heard some o' the sheepmen were left chewin' dirt,' Barrow continued after a moment's consideration. 'We got to wonderin' if that was the truth of it. What do you reckon, Mr Lane?'

'I reckon there's some folk in Clayburn should know better'n spurtin' long-tongue,' Burt laughed. 'Anyways, I haven't been to town lately,' he said, yielding to sincerity.

Barrow knew that was as much as he would learn. He remarked that it wasn't long until noon, and invited Burt to stay and eat.

'Thanks. It's right neighborly o' you, but I got some homely chores. An' I got to start buildin' a kennel,' he said with a smile. He walked back to the barn with Barrow, mounted the roan and tipped his hat in farewell.

'Enjoy your dogs. Remember, they'll eat bad characters, but only bark at you an' yours,' Barrow advised. 'You'll have the grain by midday tomorrow.'

9

Burt rode away from the Barrow farm, turned north, back through the creek and into the willow brakes. He was heedless of any immediate trouble when the roan threw its head and ears back, was already going to the side and down when the bullet struck. It caught him high across his front, felt like a pole hammer striking his chest as he crashed heavily to the ground.

The roan spooked away from their bearing, snorted through the willow and out into the range below Wild Meddow's home pasture.

Burt lay on his back. He was hurt and heavily winded, but he pulled his Colt, listened to the grate of his breath in the close silence. The bushwhacker was two or three hundred yards off, somewhere between where Burt lay and the house. It would be a few minutes yet, before he'd get to consider his work. Burt looked down at his chest. 'You'll pay for this shirt, goddamn you,' he cursed. 'It's a store-bought.'

In the following stillness, a distressed kingfisher darted from its perch in the willows. But Burt had already heard the sound of hoofs. It was two horses walking, two would-be killers that were coming towards him. He gauged their direction, followed the movement as he brought himself to his knees. They wouldn't have a precise bearing, and weren't yet visible through the trees. However, Burt knew the tracks of his roan were deep in the soft ground, and would be spotted any moment.

When the riders did come across the hoofmarks, Burt heard them draw rein. He scrambled sideways, made his way to the water's edge and the root bole of a craggy willow. Although he felt wetness around his middle from oozing blood, he wasn't in much pain. I guess I'd be dead if it was a killing wound, he thought. A moment later, he heard the riders again when they started talking.

'I'm tellin' you, Tex, he's got to be lyin' here somewhere,' a voice faltered. 'The horse couldn't o' run that far.'

Burt recognized the voice of Rush Pleasants, remembered the threat he'd made, the last time he'd seen him.

'All these goddamn trees look the same, up close,' the man called Tex, answered back. 'An' how'd you know you hit him, even?'

'I saw him. He went down like a stuck buffler.'

'Beware the wounded,' Burt mouthed silently and took a deep breath.

The two men shifted their horses cautiously through the timber, kept their distance from the creek. Burt eased himself up from behind the knot of tangled roots to have a look. Now he could see that the man with Pleasants was another one of Dodgson and Maber's crew. He was called Texas Smollet, and Burt recognized him from Lefty Detes.

Burt let his breath out, hoped they'd come near enough for him to take them both down. It was the threat he'd used on Pleasants, and what he wanted to do. But they didn't get any closer. They were so sure about where Burt had fallen, they were pulling their horses round in tight circles.

'I ain't steppin' down into this stuff,' he heard Pleasants say. 'There'll likely be snakes in here, or some other slimy varmints.'

'Yeah, all sorts. An' Lane would be throwin' lead at us, if he was still kickin'.'

'Let's vamoose,' Pleasants decided. 'We'll tell Cole and Vaughn it's safe to walk on in. If them Meddow beeves are left much longer, they'll get so swollen with lard, they'll bust wide open.'

Burt gritted his teeth until his jawbone ached. The only reason he had for letting his assailants go was to stay alive, and he wondered darkly if it was good enough. The men had obviously been to his house, and spotted him coming up from the south through the creek. That meant that cold-cocking him was just about their only safe option. But he did have the advantage of them not knowing they'd blown it, and sometime it was going to cost them real dear.

Burt made his way to where the willow broke on to the open range land. Ahead of him was his house, and he hunkered down for a moment, cursed gently as he held his arms around his middle. There was no sign of Pleasants and Smollet, and he guessed they were probably riding to the stock lane before going on up to Clayburn. He wondered whether there were any more sheepmen or their gunnies around, if they had a lookout placed, in case he survived.

Burt clawed some thin shards of bark from the tree beside him. He spat and kneeded them into a soft wad, tentatively pushed it through the tear in his shirt. 'Where's a goddamn physic pusher when you need him,' he muttered, but knew that the willow contained a valuable medicinal property.

After a painful half hour's walk, Burt saw his ranch house shimmering in the afternoon's heat. He heard a soft snort on the breeze and turned back to see his roan was making ground on him. It was still nervy though, and walked in its own good time.

There didn't appear to be anyone around the ranch or its outbuildings, but Burt waited another fifteen minutes. The wound was still aching dully, and he felt shaky, but he held on to the horn of his saddle, circled wide to the sheds at the rear of the house. It was now late in the afternoon, and other than the scuffling of his corralled riding stock, there was still no other movement.

As he dragged the saddle off the roan, he saw the

boot prints behind the barn. It looked like two riders had paid a visit, showed that Pleasants and Smollet had had a good look around.

From a fire he'd made in the scullery, Burt heated up a kettle of water. He cleaned his wound, was satisfied that it was nothing more than a flesh wound. 'My pa would o' said it was more blood than bother,' he muttered. Struggling into a large, no-frills hickory shirt, he went to get his rifle from the barn. He noticed some disinfectant among the animal ointments he'd purchased at the mercantile, thought a dash of pungent carbolic on top of the willow dressing might help him along.

Back in the house, he was going to cook a meal, but he began to feel sick as fatigue gripped him. Cradling the rifle, he lay down on a cot outside of the scullery, and closed his eyes.

It was close to midnight when Burt woke. He reeled to the front door and threw the bolts, saw the immense awning of stars across the darkness of the valley.

His chest was tight, and he was sore, but the bad pain had subsided. Not feeling particularly hungry, he went back to make coffee and open a can of sweet, condensed milk. With the first of three spoonsful he smiled wistfully, tried to think of one of his father's axioms that wasn't connected with the eating of food or manfully bearing an injury.

Reflecting on what he'd heard earlier, Burt

reckoned that Pleasants had meant the sheepmen could occupy Wild Meddow at their leisure, so it wouldn't necessarily be that night, or even the next day. With Burt's bones already being stripped out by the creek, Dodgson and Maber could stroll in. And, free from the fear of attack, they'd fetch the sheep. But that could be another mistake, allow Burt the time to think about defending his ranch.

He went to his bedroom and heeled off his boots, spooned more of the rich, desirous milk, before succumbing to another sleep.

The rising sun slanted through the easterly facing windows. It was near eight o'clock when Burt climbed achily from his bed. He cursed at the stiffness, tentatively flexed his neck and arms.

He rekindled the fire and gave his wound some more attention. To his relief, there was no fresh bleeding, and using the carbolic, he carefully fashioned a clean dressing. Then he munched on one of Ruse Barrow's carrots, mused on a more proper and fitting breakfast.

An hour later, he sorted himself a sure-foot mare and rode out to where the Meddow family burial plot was sited. The rising ground offered a watchful sweep from the Springfield Hogback in the west to near the Bighorn River in the east.

Nothing except his small herd of grazing cattle moved across the land. But, just before noon, two wagons emerged from the timber on the near side of

Gray Bull Creek. True to his word, Ruse Barrow was bringing his grain in.

'Got myself some canine company,' Burt said, but not in an altogether convinced way. He gently heeled the mare from the shady grove of beech trees, and went to meet his visitors.

10

The two dogs and their pups were on the first wagon that was driven by Ruse Barrow. As they crossed the home pasture, Burt rode alongside and bade them all good day, nodded at the farmer's two sons who were driving the second wagon.

'You got a big family,' he cordially suggested to Barrow.

'Yeah. In my life, everythin' seems to come in two's. Everythin' except days o' rest, that is,' Barrow answered, noticing that every now and again Burt took a look back at the creek. 'Someone followin'?' he asked.

'No, not exactly followin'. They've been an' gone,' Burt replied, the pain still taut across his ribs.

Out front of the barn, Barrow levered the brake, nodded back towards the dogs. 'You watch out now. An' don't smile ... they see your teeth an' think you're goin' for *them*. For Pete's sake, never get bit. Don't even look 'em in the eye just yet. The dog's Samson, an' we call the bitch Delia.'

'Not Delilah?' Burt asked with a quizzical smile.

'I already told you, they're faithful,' Barrow said and returned the smile. 'I can tell you took rain checks on Sunday School.'

Burt didn't understand why the names mattered, but as he dismounted he realized what was happening. Unless Barrow was bringing part of the blood litter along for a ride, it looked like he was about to take on the whole bulldog family. He wondered again if Barrow was more slippy than he looked, if now he'd want more than the twenty dollars Burt had paid for the pups.

The dogs were leashed securely on top of the sacked grain. They both gave throaty growls and laid back their ears when Burt approached.

'Stand off some. Let 'em get used to you. . . . your whiff,' Barrow advised.

Burt sniffed anxiously and moved around to the back of the wagon. He reached tentatively for the pups, shuddered at the mother's warning snarl. He took a deep breath, cursed silently when he saw the stretch of the rawhide leashes. Then he scooped up the pups, and with one under each arm, carried them to the house.

Outside of his scullery, Burt stared at the cot he'd used for a few hours the previous evening. Kick by kick, he moved it to near the door of his bedroom, where he gently lay down the drowsy pups. Then he pared some shin of beef, looked around for suitable dishes.

When he went back to the wagons, Burt found the Barrows had already unloaded and were packing the sacks into the barn.

'You goin' to tote mister an' missus now,' one of the boys said.

Burt thought he detected mischief, and he threw Ruse Barrow a fitting glance. But he'd already decided that he wasn't going to split up the dog family.

After a nerve-racking minute, he carefully unfastened the rope from around Delia's neck. 'They're asleep!' he shouted as the mother bounded straight from the wagon to the house.

Samson's body muscle rippled, and from one side of its mouth, an upper lip curled above a spiky canine.

'Huh, no danger o' me smilin' back at that,' Burt said, and untied the leash from the running rail of the wagon. Samson jumped to the ground at his feet, and Burt quickly grabbed the leash, held the dog tight until he got inside the house.

Delia was sniffing around her pups, nosing them aside to make her own cot space. Burt let Samson go, stood watching the proceedings as it quartered the small room of its new home.

Burt pushed two platters of meat across the floor, and without fuss backed off. He closed the door and returned to help the Barrows finish the stockpiling of his grain. Fifteen minutes later, they were all sitting around the kitchen table, dunking crackers in strapping coffee.

'It looks like them sheepmen *are* headin' this way,' Ruse Barrow remarked, but there was nothing implicit in his voice.

Burt eyed him speculatively. 'Well, you could be crossin' the Potomac an' headed this way. It's *how far* away they are, that interests me.'

'They're around the Pikes,' Barrow responded. 'Right now, they're pushin' two big flocks an' a covered wagon through the west end of Ankle Iron.'

Burt looked part interested. 'That's Brew Carron's problem,' he said. 'Is that why you didn't tell me before?'

Barrow shook his head. 'No, I didn't necessarily want to create trouble where there ain't none. But pretty soon, there's only goin' to be the south creek between you, so I been thinkin' there might be somethin' prudent in the mention.'

'Like what?' Burt asked.

'Like, they're runnin' with a couple o' fellers who tote silver badges.'

Burt groaned testily as he got a more complete picture. One of Barrow's boys who'd seen the move reckoned the sheep could reach the crossing along Gray Bull Creek before nightfall, that it was obvious the sheep were being safeguarded by law officers.

'Yeah, if they weren't, Ankle Iron or Single Rig would have thumped 'em the minute they'd reached cattle range,' Burt suggested knowingly.

'Thumped 'em *again*, you mean,' Barrow said.

Burt half smiled, almost agreed. So Dodgson and Maber could march on to his land believing he wasn't there to defend it. No doubt Pleasants and Smollet had put it to them that Burt Lane was fish feed.

'How do them dogs o' mine feel about sheep?' he asked. 'I'm interested, 'cause if anyone decides to make a move on Wild Meddow, they're all the help I got.'

In shifting a heavy sack around, Burt's wound had partly opened. He grimaced when he looked down, saw a ribbon of fresh blood had squeezed across his chest. He muttered something about temperature dropping, before pulling on a bleached duster.

It was late afternoon when the Barrows went to rehitch their teams. Burt went with them, rode most way to the creek, before bidding them farewell.

'Got to get better informed, get me a good look at them sheep,' he said matter-of-factly. 'You brought good grain an' I thank you for it. By the way, I'm namin' them pup boys Cain an' Abel. Ride out an' see 'em some time.'

Barrow waved. 'Hah, you really don't know your scriptures, do you, boy?' he called out. 'Maybe I'll pass by, after you've burned up some mutton.'

'That'll be up to them,' Burt shouted back. But he was still wondering what sort of deal he'd got with the dogs.

Burt waited for the Barrows' wagons to ford the creek, then he followed on. He waited by the fallen willow until almost first dark. It was only then that he saw the roil of dust from the approaching sheep. They were in two main flocks, the furthest still a long way off. The leaders were headed his way, hugging the broken timber along the south fork. There was a covered wagon, with four saddled horses tied alongside. The riders were resting with their backs to the wheels, apparently talking.

Burt knew that to get sheep that far, it would have taken good reason and high-ranking law officers. The two that Ruse Barrow had seen would be deputy US marshals at the least. Burt quit the timber, heeled the roan into a canter for the wagon.

He'd covered half the distance when, from his right, a line of riders stepped their horses from the creekside willows. Burt knew immediately it was Brewster Carron and his crew. They'd probably have dogged the sheep near all the way from Elk Valley, then across the western sector of Ankle Iron land. They'd remained well hidden in the foothills of the Pikes, else the Barrows would have seen them.

Although they'd been aware of Burt ever since he'd emerged from the timber, not a man moved from alongside the sheep wagon. He rode closer, nudged his roan alongside the tethered horses.

He nodded at the four men, guessed that two of them were sheepmen's hired guns. The other two wore wide-brimmed hats and had deputy US marshal's badges pinned to their coats. One of them looked inscrutably at Burt, the other seemed slightly irritated. He got to his feet slowly, wanted to threaten by his size.

'You lookin' for somethin', mister?' he wanted to know. 'I thought we told you cowboys to stay away from these parts.'

'I'd o' remembered if you'd told *me* somethin' like that,' Burt challenged. 'I'm lookin' to find out where them sheep are headed.'

'Land twixt the creeks. They already tried it once, but got 'emselves shot up. But now they got us to look out for 'em. You look kind o' bewildered,' the marshal added, his eyes narrowing as he started to wonder about Burt.

'I ain't bewildered, Marshal. I'm riled ... wonderin' why the law's aidin' an' abettin' a bunch o' goddamn maggots that are about to raze my land.'

11

The other marshal raised himself from the ground, stood shoulder to shoulder with his partner.

'I'm John Coulson,' an' that's Harry Defe,' he said, attempting to read Burt's intent. 'An' as far as we're concerned, the land's owned by Cole Dodgson. It was him an' Vaughn Maber who came to Clover City for enforcement. That's *us* an' what *we're* doin' here. Now, just who the hell are *you?*'

'Burton Lane. Supposin' there's a difference, Marshal, are you workin' for the owner o' Wild Meddow, or have you got a personal deal goin' with Dodgson?' Burt asked.

'*Nothin's* personal with us,' Defe scowled out quickly 'We come to protect the owner o' the land. See to it they get their rights.'

'Glad to hear it, but perhaps you ain't yet understood what I just told you. Wild Meddow belongs to *me*. You're lettin' them shiny badges draw you the wrong way,' Burt threw back.

The marshals were momentarily troubled, were looking to each other for a new approach, when the two gunmen scrambled to their feet and shouted a warning.

From the creekside timber, the Ankle Iron crew were approaching at the gallop. The marshals saw them, turned quickly to see that Cole Dodgson was already leading a large band of men from the opposite direction. Riding with them was Texas Smollet and Rush Pleasants. Both men were agitated as they approached, but it was Dodgson that revealed an immediate annoyance at the sight of Burt.

Calmly, Coulson and Defe drew carbines from their saddle boots, walked forward to meet the Ankle Iron men.

'Bite on it, Carron. Stay put,' Defe called out. 'We're empowered to bring you down, if we have to.'

'We're supportin' Burt Lane,' Carron answered. 'He's a cowman, if it ain't already clear.'

His face set hard with anger, Cole Dodgson kicked his horse forward. 'We need to run sheep, Marshal,' he shouted. 'I've seen this drifter in Clayburn,' he added, indicating Burt with his thumb. 'What's he doin' here?'

'That was somethin' we was findin' out, when you hell-raisers arrived,' Coulson replied coolly. Then he faced Burt. 'Do you know this man?' he asked.

'I know *about* him,' Burt said. 'An' the reason he wants to know what I'm doin' here is because not much more'n a day ago, he thought he'd slooped me down to the Bighorn. Me standin' here must be a real big surprise for him an' his hirelings.'

'Hah, the man's been too long without a hat,' Dodgson blustered. 'Are you officers gettin' my sheep movin' or not?'

Not one to be harried, Coulson looked to Burt. 'With what you just been claimin', mister, you're certainly stokin' a tale or two,' he said long-sufferingly. 'Why'd he need to get you wasted?'

'So's he could make his move on to Wild Meddow a lot easier. That's why, goddammit. Why don't you turn your thoughts to them two sittin' nice an' quiet behind him? Ask 'em if they know why the hell I'm carryin' a raw gunshot wound under this duster,' Burt answered snappily.

'If that's right, you'll be wantin' to make a charge against 'em,' Defe butted in. 'You'll have to prove it, o' course, an' back in Clover City.'

'Oh, there's another way, Marshal. I just ain't thought it out yet.'

'Yeah, an' you best make sure I ain't around when you do,' Coulson advised drily. 'Now, what was it you were tellin' us about this property between the creeks?' he asked.

'I own it, an' I got my own cattle in there,' Burt explained pithily.

Dodgson was infuriated. 'I've had enough o' this,' he raged. 'Let's move.'

Coulson shook his head, and glared. 'That's now *two* people questionin' your right to that land, Mr

73

Dodgson. This mornin' I listened to some character sayin' it was doubtful you own nary a sod. I reckon to get this sorted ... to avoid any more misunderstandin' ... we really should see some proof o' your title,' he suggested helpfully.

'For chris'sakes, my deed papers were good enough for the judge in Clover City,' Dodgson blurted angrily. 'An' good enough to get *you* out here. What the hell do you want to see 'em again for? Anyways, they're in Clayburn. You don't think I'd be stupid enough to be carryin' em out here, do you?'

Coulson took a deep breath, turned his attention back to Burt. 'What he says is true enough, an' it makes sense,' he suggested as evenly as he could.

'No it don't,' Burt disputed. 'I've already got a heap of investment up there ... family plot you might say. He's pullin' a big hank o' that sheep wool over your eyes, Marshal. Him takin' over my land and my house really ain't makin' sense to me.'

Coulson gave a cruel smile. 'Well, the way I see it, he's got the advantage o' the moment, sort o' got the drop on all of us.'

'No, Marshal, I've already said he don't,' Burt said. 'An' if you're genuinely interested in enforcin' the rights o' the land owner, then I suggest you cast your eyes over this.'

When Coulson saw Burt reach beneath his duster, he handed his carbine to Defe. The marshal then moved alongside the roan to take the fold of papers that Burt handed him. In the failing light, he leafed through them, ran a thumb over the dark smudge of blood. One was a receipt for goods purchased at the mercantile store in Clayburn, the other had two, small red wax seals in a bottom corner. It was a certified scrip from the General Land Office in Washington. Appended was a personal letter written and signed by Noble Rockford. It read:

This letter testifies that Burt Lane has been known to me [the undersigned Noble Rockford] for many years. For the last five of them he has been foreman of the Noble Rockford Ranch. During this time he has accepted Rockford heifers – including four Poll Durhams – in lieu of a seventy-five cent on the dollar wage. He is leaving my employ to take his herd of cattle south to the homestead property known as Wild Meddow. I wish to make clear to all interested parties that Burt Lane has always proved to be an honest and law-abiding citizen. Any appropriate help afforded him will be well met by me. Furthermore, dispensation will be commensurate and dispatched for any wilful act of harm or hindrance.

Finally and to whom it may concern:

It may well be necessary on occasion that Burt Lane has need to implement his real and proper birth name of Burton C. Meddow.

12

John Coulson took his carbine back and took a long, hard look at Burt. Harry Defe cast an eye over the letter and deed.

'Can't say I know the signature, but no one's goin' to exploit Noble Rockford's name, I do know that,' the marshal drawled. 'I'd say if they value a long an' prosperous life, they best not ignore the man's notion o' *dispensation*, eh, Mr Meddow?'

Burt nodded. 'I haven't been called that for nigh on ten years,' he said. 'But I've always owned Wild Meddow.'

Cole Dodgson spurred his horse closer, his jaw working angrily. 'Marshal, I don't figure on havin' to ask you again to get my sheep movin'. What the hell you jawin' about now?' he demanded. 'You got orders, so get on with carryin' 'em out.' Then he reached for the papers. 'Let me see what you got there,' but Defe was handing them back to Burt.

'I can get tired o' you tellin' us what to do,'

Coulson icily advised. 'An' I got somethin' else to consider. Like swearin' falsehoods to federal officers.'

'My attorneys have all the evidence needed to establish my rights. You're sellin' out to the goddamn cowmen,' Dodgson railed.

Coulson levered a shell into the chamber of his carbine. 'That's enough, Dodgson,' he barked. 'Turn your sheep an' keep off Ankle Iron range. Don't come back, you hear?' Dodgson, kicked his horse, angrily wheeled it full circle. 'I ain't got this close just to turn back,' he yelled. 'We'll move 'em down to the creek water, an' we'll settle in court.'

'If any one o' you so much as gets his toes wet, I'll deputize every goddamn cowboy within shoutin' range an' run you up an' over the Rockies. You goddamn hear me?'

'An' I got family that'll help establish my rights. They'll bite your goddamn asses,' Burt contributed enthusiastically.

The muscles in Dodgson's face and neck trembled with suppressed fury as he saw his time in the valley was up. He cursed and raked his horse's flanks with his spurs. The Ankle Iron crew grinned their scorn as he waved his men back towards the sheep.

The deputy marshals untied and mounted their horses, rode between Carron and Burt. John Coulson studied the owner of Wild Meddow.

'With some folk it's all a matter o' timin'. Some have it, some don't,' he said drily. 'You turnin' up

77

when you did must o' sure frustrated Dodgson an' Maber . . . given 'em an' overridin' wish for killin'. They would o' been hopin' to make some sort o' squatters' claim.'

'Serves 'em right. Wishin' an' hopin' an' what's legal ain't the same thing,' Carron said, a touch haughtily. 'I told you this mornin', Dodgson and Maber don't own diddly squat.'

'But the Clover City judge was given *some sort* o' evidence by Dodgson's lawyers. An' *I* never saw bona-fide papers,' Coulson claimed. 'If Dodgson and his sheep had got 'emselves on to Wild Meddow, it would o' dragged through the Sheridan courts. Probably taken years to sort out, an' Dodgson knew it.'

'Yeah, probably ended up ownin' it too,' Burt furthered. 'But I'm in now, for as long as I can stay alive.'

Carron was curious. 'You're one o' the Meddow family?' he asked. 'A cousin or somethin'?'

Burt shook his head, gave a delayed smile. 'Conrad Meddow was my father. I was the one who survived the sheep war o' ten years ago' . . . the *only* one. They rustled an' killed all our cattle. I got away . . . hid up on the Hogback. I thought they'd come after me, but they never did. They got scared at what they'd done an' scuttled for the border. I didn't know all o' that, an' rode north. I paid a settler to do the buryin'.'

Coulson, Defe and Carron walked their horses

steadily forward as they listened, and Burt continued.

'From that day to this, all I've planned an' waited for was to come back to Wild Meddow,' he told them. 'I never thought I'd run up against another sheepman. What sort o' bad luck's that, eh?' Burt, rattled through the rest of the story as though he was sloughing off bitterness like an old skin.

It was Brewster Carron that voiced an opinion. 'Well, you came back. I reckon we could afford you some help after ten years. Dodgson an' Maber won't be goin' south to graze, *or* to the Sheridan courts. They'll be back.'

'Why not give *me* them papers,' Coulson said supportively. 'I can turn them over to the US marshal. As far as anyone movin' on to your range is concerned, you'll be indemnified. No marshal or judge is goin' to act for anyone else, when you got the proof locked away in a Clover City bank. An' you can have a copy made to keep in Clayburn.'

Burt decided that although hard-boiled, both marshals were fundamentally honest. It was a helpful offer from Coulson, and Burt thanked him. There was an original deed issue recorded in a Wyoming land registry office, and had been for more than twenty years, ever since his father acquired the land. But now it didn't matter too much, and Burt didn't know of its exact whereabouts.

He separated the deed from the mercantile goods receipt, and handed it back to the deputy marshal. 'I'm obliged,' he said. 'At least now it's a Meddow asset, whether I'm dead or alive.'

Coulson smiled. 'I'll mention it to Warner Herrick. He can inform the town marshal. But now we got to shepherd them sheep while we can still see 'em. There's too many places for 'em to hide if they get into the foothills.'

The men shook hands. Without another word, Coulson and Defe snapped their mounts into a canter, headed south-west to the slopes of the Needle Pikes.

'Neither o' *them* marshals is goin' to ride easy after bein' gulled by Maber an' Dodgson,' Carron remarked.

'Well, they got to offer protection for a mile or two yet. They don't want anyone to be at the mercy of Ankle Iron, do they, Mr Carron?' Burt suggested mischievously.

Carron accepted the comment with a dry smile. 'For a while there, I figured we were deep into the treacle,' he said. 'But you ain't got the tang o' sheep on you, an' maybe I should o' knowed better. Were you sayin' that Dodgson's men were tryin' to kill you?'

Burt told Carron about how Pleasants and Texas Smollet had attempted to remove him from Dodgson's plan for Wild Meddow.

'That's a curiously benevolent sort o' revenge . . . lettin' 'em ride away,' Carron suggested.

'They'll be back,' Burt said confidently. 'You said so yourself.'

80

Most of the Ankle Iron crew had fanned out to keep a watchful eye on the sheep flocks. Carron yelled for two of the back riders. 'Pitt, you an' Macey's takin' up lodgin' at Wild Meddow for a few days. If you even get a whiff o' mutton, take a string, an' ride 'em hard.'

Carron's cowboys waved their acknowledgement, rode fast to select the saddle mounts. It was timely support and Burt wasn't against their company. Under the blanket of darkness, the three men then rode for the creek timber and the crossing to Wild Meddow. Not for the first time since midday, Burt considered the interests of his dogs and called on the roan for speed.

13

The dogs were quick learners. On returning to the house, Burt was allowed to rumple the pups. Then Samson and Delia ran off to the barn to get acquainted with Pitt and Macey, grant them the familiarity that led to access. Later, Burt pushed open the door to his bedroom, indicated to Samson that there was a saddle blanket at the foot of his bed.

But in spite of the security offered by his dogs, Burt didn't rest or sleep that night. In the morning he could hardly move. He was tentatively applying a clean dressing to his chest wound when Pitt and Macey walked into the house. Pitt sucked air through his teeth, shook his head.

'That ain't too fetchin'. Reckon you need to see a doctor,' he said. 'You got a buggy or a wagon out there somewhere?'

'If I *do* decide to see some town sawbones, I'll make it on the roan, thank you.' Toughing it out, Burt buttoned up his shirt. 'It's sore an' stiff, just like an' old bullet scuff should be.'

Pitt and Macey shared a meaningful look, thought better of voicing further concern.

'Anyways, I don't much like the idea o' leavin' you two here alone,' Burt added.

Pitt smiled. 'It's *you* the sheepmen want,' the cowboy warned good humouredly. 'It won't do 'em any good to harm Macey or me. If they think otherwise, one of us'll make it back to Ankle Iron.'

The tight soreness in Burt's chest didn't ease off as he hoped it would. After some breakfast, he actually felt worse, broke into the sweat of a mounting fever. He accepted the need for him to see a doctor, gritted his teeth while saddling the roan.

Once over the north creek, he took the stock trail that ran around Yearling Timms's Red Ribbon ranch. He held the mare to a lope for fear of falling from the saddle, so it was close to sundown when he saw the twin windmills of Clayburn ahead of him. He put the roan into the stable, then took a room at the town's boarding house. It was approaching full dark when he asked where he'd find the doctor.

Digby Quill, MD, rolled the end of a cigar around his mouth. 'If you'd got yourself a little closer, maybe he'd o' shot a few ribs out,' he observed drily. He swabbed the wound, dusted some yellow powder to Burt's chest and applied a fresh dressing. 'You don't look like the kind o' feller who'll rest up, but if you don't, the sepsis might take hold, an' *that* ain't a good diagnosis,' he advised. He handed over a small bottle of laudanum. 'Find yourself a bed, an' drink half o' this. No more.'

Burt felt sick and his head was throbbing, couldn't do much else other than go along with the doctor's advice. Back in his room, he swallowed the laudanum and lay down fully dressed. He doused the bedside lamp, and ten minutes later drifted into an exhausted sleep.

The next day was well along when he awoke. He had a cautious stretch, and washed, noticed a low, reassuring growl from his stomach. Descending the stairs, he crossed the small lobby and went out on to the sidewalk. The street was thronged with the mules, oxen and horses of settlers' wagons that were being loaded with supplies. He thought he'd look for somewhere to eat and turned down the street, walked past the mercantile store and into Fraser Brax.

The newspaper publisher hesitated, before smiling a greeting. 'D'you remember me, Fraser Brax?' he asked. 'We met at Lefty Detes, the day you set down here. I was hopin' to see you again. Would you mind comin' back to the office for a few minutes?'

Burt did remember him, but it was mainly because of Brax's daughter that he agreed to walk on to the office of the *Clayburn Tidings*.

Inside the glass-panelled building, Brax stopped beside the cluttered desk where his daughter was checking copy.

'This is my daughter, Hester,' he said.

'Have we met?' Hester asked, smiling uncertainly.

Burt could have said it was outside of the saloon, but he didn't. 'Perhaps. But you'd think I'd have a better memory of it,' he offered as a more valuable and winning response.

'I recall you sayin' your name was Burt Lane,' Brax said, while he checked the tip of a new pencil. 'But it's actually Burt Meddow, an' you're the beneficiary o' Wild Meddow.'

'Is that some sort of accusation?' Burt asked of him.

'Not at all. It's corroboration . . . another way of askin' a question. It's a newsman's trick. I *also* heard the sheep got pretty close to your land.'

'Hmm. Now *that* definitely sounds like a question,' Burt said. 'Also sounds like the makin's of a front-page story,' Burt answered, hoping it tied up the matter.

But Brax wanted a lot more than that. 'There's a story behind you, Mr Meddow. So why don't we talk about it for a while,' he suggested. 'We're both law-abidin' citizens. For what it's worth, I'm considerin' the settlers along Gray Bull Creek. They ain't got much of a voice, not one you'd hear from out there. A range war will ruin 'em . . . wipe 'em out. So maybe words that I can make available will help, the pen bein' mightier than the sword an' all that.'

For a moment, Burt pondered on Brax's rhetoric.

'Well, I don't know what I can say to help,' he said, not knowing what kind of story was required. 'I remember when we were kids, our ma an' pa took up sections in the valley. There was some unwanted surplus railroad land and Pa bought it with a couple of vacated claims. He wanted most everything between the north an' south creeks. He said it was a place where we'd be safe.'

Brax nodded at the palpable sting of bitterness in Burt's voice. 'I understand. Please go on,' he said, continuing with his notes.

'My ma died o' smallpox, an' we buried her on the ranch. Soon after that was when Ike Plummer's sheep outfit moved into the Pikes. They were to the south an' west of us, an' trouble started right off. Pa refused to sell up, so our cattle were raided. Some were killed, the rest run off. That's when the Plummers used their goddamn sheep. They ran 'em across the creek, straight on to Wild Meddow. We fought 'em for a time though, an' a bunch never made it back out o' the valley. They're the one's who's still there . . . in their bone yard.'

Burt nodded his thanks to Hester, who placed a mug of strong coffee in front of him.

'Old man Plummer grabbed what men he could, an' came right back. Pa packed me off to hide in the willows along the north creek. My brother was supposed to come with me, but he didn't. He wanted to help Pa, an' they killed him too.'

Brax took a deep breath and slowly shook his

head. 'You were on your own then?' he asked considerately.

'Yeah, on my very own. Weren't even a goddamn rooster for company. I got help from a farmer who told me he was goin' to move on. He set up the headstones, then later brought me out in his wagon. I think he'd been a long-time friend o' my parents.'

'You must have had *some* money?' Brax pressed with a little more professional attention.

'Yeah, there was a family reserve. Ma always said it was for if disaster struck. It was enough to get us all back east, schoolin' for me an' taxes paid. The next year, I got work up north, eventually made it to the Rockford ranch. Over the years, I got to be ramrod an' gained some stock. I guess there'll be a few others keen to fill in the rest o' the story,' Burt suggested when he'd finished.

The newspaperman made a wry smile. 'There's facts an' there's myths, Mr Meddow. But it's a fact I need some shadin' for next week's issue.'

'A few big windies, you mean. Well, I'm sorry to disappoint you, Mr Brax, but that's all I've got. I ain't no dime-store novel writer,' Burt insisted. He was going to say he took a bullet, was carrying a chest wound, but in the circumstances thought it best to restrain the drama. 'I took a fall, near the creek. That's what I'm doin' here in town . . . seein' the doc. Now, if you'll excuse me, I'm hungry, an' need me some breakfast.'

Brax was still not going to be put off. He went off

again with his persuasive talk, but Hester interrupted to save him from Burt's growing irritation.

'Mr Meddow's right, Pa', she said. 'An' you know better than to take a man too far away from his grub.' She paused, smiled supportively at Burt. 'Would you mind if I accompany you? It seems like *yesterday* morning that I had *my* breakfast.'

'Be my guest,' Burt replied, thinking he'd have to find an alternative to the basic fixings he'd had in mind. He turned to Brax. 'I've been Burt Lane for a good many years, an' the name's kind o' stuck. If you don't mind, I'd like to leave it that way,' he said.

14

Hester knew of an eating place not far along from the newspaper offices, and she suggested that they take a seat there. From a list of meals that favored beef, Burt went for stew. Hester had her coffee, didn't say much until she saw Burt contemplating the gravy that sat darkly on this plate.

'Well, what do you normally do with it?' she asked with a smile.

Burt smiled and soaked it up with half a sourdough biscuit.

Hester wanted to get a conversation going and asked about the Wild Meddow.

Burt described the spread and what it meant to him. For a minute or so he surprised himself with a near emotional description.

'I'd like to see it someday,' Hester responded, as they stepped back out on to the sidewalk.

'Yeah, combine it with tellin' me somethin' about you,' Burt said, looking pleased. 'Fair's fair.'

Brax wasn't in the office when they returned. Burt hung up his hat, and Hester spread a recent previous issue of the *Tidings* across a copy desk. Almost the whole of the front page was devoted to news of the sheep and cattle war. Much of it was speculation, but there was no doubt of an editor's trail as Brax hammered on about the plight of blameless settlers along Gray Bull Creek. He said it was inevitable that it would be the innocents who would suffer the worst and most.

Burt placed a finger in the middle of the last column. 'Yeah, there's the guts of it,' he muttered. Then the nerve in the corner of his eye twitched. 'If the settlers do suffer, it'll mean sheepmen have moved back on to Wild Meddow . . . that for one real bad reason I won't be there,' he continued solemnly.

Hester saw that Burt was deeply troubled. She was about to ask about it, if he could see any future, when the bell over the door rang. Her father and Warner Herrick entered the office.

The sheriff was carrying a scattergun which he laid along the coat hooks inside the door. He nodded recognition at Burt. 'How you doin', feller,' he said. 'I heard about the meetin' you had with Coulson an' Defe. They rode back to Clover City while I've been ridin' the mail stage. I thought I'd run a lawful eye over the situation, as it were. The lid's restin' snug enough right now, but if it looks like comin' off, I'll recommend some support for Pruett.'

'We got some news regardin' *your* property . . . Wild

Meddow,' Brax said.

Herrick nodded. 'That's right. Dodgson's lawyer says him an' Maber were claimin' rights of unworked land. It's a hard one to prove, though. An' Maber suggested they might take legal action for what happened to 'em.'

'Huh, makes you wonder what side the law's on,' Brax said scathingly.

'It often works in wondrous ways,' Herrick chuckled gruffly and turned to Burt. 'Can you give me a minute?' he asked, and walked to the back of the office. He stepped into a small composing room, out of the sight of Hester and her father.

'Has it occurred to you that you're some sort o' firebrand here?' he asked.

'You suggestin' I apologize for any inconvenience caused, Sheriff?' Burt retorted after a moment's hesitation. 'Maybe suggestin' I turn a cheek on this . . . my back?'

Herrick shook his head good-naturedly. 'No, not a bit of it. I want you to stay alive. But you know as well as I do them sheep ain't goin' to stay south o' the creek for long. Irrespective o' the rights an' wrongs of it, you're goin' to be in the way.'

Burt leaned in close to the sheriff. 'Well, *I'm* the rights an' *they're* the wrongs, goddamnit,' he snapped. 'If you want innocent folk to stay alive, give *them* the attention your goddamn law's been heapin' on to Dodgson an' Maber. I'm only lookin' out for what's mine. What about you? Who the hell *are* you supportin' here?'

'I told you, I'm supportin' you. But *you* ain't thinkin' about the longer term,' Herrick replied. 'Have you thought o' what happens to Wild Meddow if you get yourself killed?' he asked.

'About the same as if I *don't*, it sounds like,' Burt reacted quickly.

'O' course, if you had someone to leave it to, no sheep would ever get to leave its sign on the land. That's a certainty, an' that goes for the likes o' Dodgson too. This has always been cow country. You can make sure it stays that way.'

Burt turned around and looked through to the office. He saw that Brax and Hester were doing a poor job of not listening, and he allowed them a spare smile. 'Makes it pretty pointless shootin' me,' he answered Herrick. 'Is one o' them wills you pen yourself acceptable in court?'

'Yeah, they are in Wyoming.'

'In that case, I'll get one written up. I'm obliged to you, Sheriff,' Burt said.

Herrick's face was inscrutable as he followed Burt back to Brax's writing desk. Burt had already noticed the ink pots, paper and pens. He moved aside the news sheet, sat down and smoothed a sheet of foolscap. Shielding his writing with one arm, he wrote the date, thoughtfully filled nearly half of one page. Five minutes later he doubled over the part he'd written, signed beneath it and took it to the sheriff who was talking with Brax and Hester.

'If you'll just witness that it's my signature, an' writ in Wyomin',' Sheriff,' he asked.

Herrick took the pen from Burt, wrote his full name alongside Burt's. 'It needs another,' he said, and handed the paper to Hester.

'Could your pa do that?' Burt interrupted. 'Gives it a kind o' weight, with him bein' the editor an' all. Sorry, Hester,' he added with a touch of unease.

'That's all right,' she chirped up. 'I'm wonderin' how much trouble could be avoided if *everyone* wrote one o' these.'

'At the moment, it's more like how much is bein' made,' Herrick rumbled.

'What would I know about anythin'?' she remarked jokily. 'I'll just attend to the chores.'

Brax shook his head and smiled at his daughter. He opened a drawer of his desk, gave Burt an envelope. 'Where're you goin' to keep it?' he asked.

'I was hopin' *you* could look after it. I won't really be the person needin' to open it.'

Brax nodded, took back the envelope and wrote something in the top corner. Then he looked up, his face showing that he'd just thought of something else. 'I spoke to the doc earlier,' he said, looking at Burt. 'He said he'd given you enough physic to bring a buffler to its knees. I'm guessin' you didn't take it.'

'I didn't take all of it. I've been helpin' to give you a stirrin' banner.' As he spoke Burt was aware, though, that his fever was returning.

'An' we're real appreciative,' Brax replied with a

smile. 'But right now, why not take advantage o' the town bein' quiet . . . do what everyone else is doin'.'

'An' what's that?' Burt wondered.

'I don't know. But whatever it is, and for as long as it lasts, you could get your head down. You look as though you could use some shut-eye.'

Involuntarily, Burt yawned at the thought. He realized that the sheriff had probably been speculating on what he'd been seeing the doctor for, accepted it was nothing more than Burt's business. He was also concerned that Pitt and Macey would get jumpy with him being gone from the ranch for so long. 'Yeah,' he said, slow and thoughtful, 'I guess it's somethin' I ain't goin' to be forced into. An' there's nothin' more for me to do here.'

Burt thanked Brax and the sheriff, took his hat that Hester offered him. He made his way out of the offices, started along the sidewalk towards the boarding house.

15

As he walked in the street-side shadows, Burt heard movement from an alleyway that emerged beside Lefty Detes. Then someone spoke and he stopped, took a sideways step into the street.

It was two of Rush Pleasant's partners that had been waiting for him. First off, Burt recognized the men's faces that were as mean and unclean as the last time he'd seen them.

'I said you'd regret not shootin' us, mister,' the taller of the two men threatened, stepping on to the sidewalk proper.

Burt recalled it was the one that went by the name of Pugg. 'If Dodgson's put you up to this, he must want rid o' you,' he said with a confidence he didn't feel.

Pugg shook his head. 'No, this is personal . . . nothin' to do with him. It's just between you, me an' Trove,' he scowled.

Burt knew it. What happened next would be

regardless of anyone else's command. The two men were intent on their own revenge, had been ever since Burt sent them packing across open rangeland without their boots.

Pugg quickly stepped forward, as Trove moved around behind Burt.

'Seems right funny, that now the shoe's on the *other* foot,' Pugg sneered. 'Difference is, you ain't comin' out o' the walk you're goin' on.'

Burt kept his thoughtful silence, had speculated on what was coming in behind Pugg's threat. He swung his body sideways, so that Pugg's rising knee hit him in the thigh. It was a hard blow, and Burt's left leg went instantly numb from the impact. Cursing, Pugg swung a fist at Burt's face. It smashed into his cheek as Burt tried to swing his head out of the way. It sent his hat flying, mashing the inside of his cheek against his teeth.

As Pugg came on, Burt staggered back. He felt Trove's arms clasp tight around his chest, the hot breath on the back of his neck.

'Goddamn cowprodder,' the man grunted.

Burt knew this was a summary beating, something likely to go way beyond the normal cow town brawl. He sucked air through his teeth, and swung both his legs up into the air. Pugg lashed out another fist, but his lunge pushed Trove backwards. Pugg missed, and Burt's boots landed full and low.

Trove grunted. He crumpled around his winded belly, and Burt drove his heel down violently on the top of his foot. There was a gasp of pain, and Burt echoed the sound as he stamped again, even harder. He felt the foot bones give and he locked his fingers, drew his arms up. The bear hug was broken, and Burt broke free of Trove's arms and the dreadful pain. He hissed ferocity, turned and piled a short, savage blow into the man's stomach. Then, without hesitation he stepped forward and punched him full-fisted in the mouth. The teeth broke apart, and the back of Trove's head crashed into a corner post of the saloon.

But now Pugg was on his feet and charging back at Burt. His arms were whirling and his face was contorted with uncontrolled rage. Burt dropped his shoulder and the man's momentum pitched him headlong into the slumped body of his partner.

Burt stepped back as Pugg landed in a mash of arms and legs. 'I'm supposed to be takin' advantage of a quiet town,' he growled, gasping from the spread of renewed pain.

For the second time, Pugg got unsteadily to his feet. 'You will be in a minute,' he said, dragging a Colt from the waistband at the rear of his pants.

Pugg was never going to be fast enough, though, and Burt was ready. He lashed the knuckles of his right hand sideways into Pugg's wrist, then back again into his grimy face. He stepped away as blood burst from Pugg's nose. Then, as he cursed his misfortune, Clayburn and everything to do with sheep, he heard the thump of running boots on the sidewalk close behind him.

'I hope they ain't close associates o' theirs,' he wheezed in between more cursing.

But it was Sheriff Herrick, and he had the scattergun in his right hand. 'I'll take him. Don't pull your gun,' he called to Burt as he swung up the twin barrels.

Pugg's face was a mask of slimy blood as he got to his feet. He raised his Colt for another go at Burt, dragged the hammer fully back. His finger was tightening on the trigger as Burt threw himself from the sidewalk.

The two shots were fired almost simultaneously, but the blast from Herrick's gun overwhelmed the sound of Pugg's Colt. Without breaking stride, the sheriff was hauling back for the next barrel.

Pugg was in mid air, hands clawing for his Colt that was already lying in the dirt of the street. There was an ominous pool of blood spread across his side and chest as he thudded into the ground. He managed to get to his knees, as his eyes clouded. A crushed lip curled back over jagged teeth. 'Still smell cow,' he spat at Burt. Then he pitched forward and died.

Herrick lowered his scattergun. 'It didn't look like he was about to surrender,' he gritted.

'No, an' he ain't the first sheepman to prefer dyin',' Burt sided with the county sheriff.

Pugg's partner was on all fours, crawling alongside the low, weatherboarding of Lefty Detes. He had a darkly-blooded and battered face, but Herrick thought he might still harbor a foolish intention.

'You do have a choice, mister,' he snarled at him. '*Mine* would be not to carry on fightin'.'

Trove tried to get up. He howled in distress, then fell sideways as the foot fractured by Burt's boot heel gave way.

'I need a doctor,' he said and let his head fall forward.

'Think yourself lucky,' Burt rasped. He looked back along the street, saw Hester Brax, before staggering into woozy darkness.

16

The liquid physic that Digby Quill had administered had done its work well. Burt opened his eyes, looked around him, then raised himself on an elbow. He had a lot of stiffness, but little pain. He reckoned that a brace of stiff whiskeys, then plenty of strong coffee, was the next stage of his healing, and he said so.

'An' how'd you propose to get from here to Lefty Detes?' Herrick observed. 'In that state of undress, I'd have to arrest you.'

Burt had a look under the sheets. 'What would you charge me with?' he asked idly.

'How about wanderin' abroad with no visible means o' support,' the sheriff jibed, and the men laughed.

Fraser Brax was looking down into the street from the window of the boarding house. 'Those sheepmen ain't goin' to cede,' he said, ominously. 'I don't care what you think, Sheriff, it ain't goin' to be a petty case o' badgerin'. Not now.'

'We'll see,' Herrick returned indifferently.

'Yeah, we will,' Brax agreed gloomily. 'Meantime, the *Tidings* has got to look to its print run,' and he waved a hand at Burt as he left the room.

'An' I'm visitin' the jailhouse,' Quill said. 'Pruett's got himself someone down there with a bad case o' lameness.'

The moment Brax returned to the office, Hester wanted to know how Burt was. 'How is he?' she asked. 'Were they Cole Dodgson's men?'

'Yeah, Pugg an' Trove,' her father replied. 'Herrick shot Pugg dead in the street, but Lane ain't hurt too bad. The doc's filled him with that snake oil of his.'

Brax sat down at his desk and pulled the foolscap to start his writing. 'We'll need some type set, Hester. I've got a top story to make up,' he said.

The lead story flowed fast from Brax's pen. He penned a thrilling account of how two murderous brutes lurked in the Clayburn shadows. How they waited to backshoot an innocent man who was half full of pain-killing medicine, a good man who was making his way through the drowsy cow town to the refuge of his sick bed.

Satisfied with his hyperbole, Brax considered a headline. He sought words that would provoke swift excitement in the townsfolk when the news sheet hit the side walk.

For the rest of the day, and through a morphine-induced sleep, Burt got the rest he needed. It was well into full dark when he pulled himself up, blinked at the oil-lit sconces along the sidewalks. The doc had administered well though, and with a heavy sigh he slumped back down from the window, slept even more soundly throughout the rest of the night.

It was still early morning when Burt lifted a hand and tugged at the blind that had been pulled sometime during the small hours. He swung his legs to the floor, sat for a few minutes and marshalled his thoughts, dredged up memories of the street fight. Then he noticed the empty laudanum bottle on the bedside table, guessed Doc Quill had paid him a visit.

He sluiced himself with cold water from a basin, and got himself dressed. He was buckling on his gunbelt, when there was a knock at the door.

'Come on in,' he called, rested the palm of his hand on the butt of his Colt.

Grif Pruett opened the door and walked in. 'Mornin',' he said, taking off his hat. 'From what I been hearin', we'd o' got to meet again before long.'

Burt nodded. 'Yeah, probably, so why this time o' day?' he said, thinking immediately it was a bit of a testy response.

'Because there's somethin' else,' Pruett said, a little uncomfortably. 'Cole Dodgson's over at Lefty Detes, an' wants to have a word with you . . . if you're well enough.'

Burt almost laughed. 'That's real funny. The man's got a sense o' humour, sendin' a town marshal to do his biddin', an' some neck. Got a bushwhacker along, has he?' he asked bitingly. 'There must be one or two that ain't yet dead or busted up.'

'He's alone. An' he came to town alone, too. He says he paid off all his hired hands. Pugg an' Trove were out for 'emselves, not workin' for him. I'm here as a peacemaker.'

Burt turned away from Pruett. He thought he might as well go and find out what Dodgson wanted, and he wasn't likely to come to much harm at Lefty Detes.

'Lead on, Marshal. Never let 'em say I was the one who wouldn't smoke the pipe,' he said, tightly.

Cole Dodgson sat at a corner table, away from the saloon's early customers. Wearing a dark suit and no spurs, it was obvious he hadn't come to town riding a horse. He gave a thin smile as the two men approached the table.

'I was wantin' this to be between you an' me,' he told Burt, his face hardening up.

'The marshal's stayin',' Burt retorted. 'As an agent o' the law, I want him to hear every word. I've got good reason to keep things in the open.'

The sheepman sniffed, threw a thoughtful glance at Pruett. 'If you're meanin' the scum that came after you yesterday, I only got back from Clover City this mornin'. Me an' Vaughn Maber have got ourselves a few herdsmen an' camp tenders, that's all.'

Burt didn't believe the man, looked around as if

he'd got something else on his mind.

'Stay a moment,' Dodgson continued. 'Take a seat an' listen to my proposal.'

'Give me one good reason why I should listen to the likes o' you,' Burt said scornfully.

Dodgson gave a small, scheming grin. 'I'll give you fifty thousand of 'em. That's a lot o' dollars for a shirt-tail plot an' a cowpen herd. What do you say, cowboy?'

'But I ain't a cowboy any longer,' Burt smiled broadly as he retaliated. 'I've suddenly become a big augur with fifty thousand dollars worth o' range land an' stock.'

Dodgson colored up threateningly as he squeezed his whiskey glass. 'I'm offerin' more than double what the place is worth, mister, an' you know it.'

'Sure, but I ain't in the business o' sellin' another cowman down the goddamn creek,' Burt continued. He turned to have a closer look at the saloon's customers. He was looking for Pleasants and Smollet, wondered why Dodgson hadn't wanted Grif Pruett to stay.

'Bein' in a small town don't mean you got to *think* small town,' Dodgson advised. 'Think about the use o' that sort o' money. We'll only be runnin' our sheep on to Wild Meddow for winter feed. The rest o' the time we'll be leasin' land south o' Needle Pikes. There'll be no eatin' of other people's grass, an' you won't be sellin' anyone down the creek, either. Whether there's any more fightin' or not's up to you.'

Burt didn't take to Dodgson's attempt at blackmail and glared icily. He wondered whether to say he'd really like to take him up on the offer, but had only just willed the land over. Instead, he smiled at the thought, turned his back and walked across to the bar.

The marshal was alongside him. 'You don't need me to point out you've just snubbed a mighty handsome offer,' he cautiously suggested.

'I'll blow the whole place apart before lettin' a single goddamn sheep graze on Wild Meddow,' Burt threatened. Then he remembered what Warner Herrick had said if the situation in the valley got any worse. 'Warner Herrick told me that if the lid comes off he'll get you support, Marshal,' he added wryly.

It dawned on him now that, other than the use of another name, the trouble was rising as it had so many years before, when the Plummer outfit moved murderously on the Meddow family.

A disturbing shudder ran through Burt's body. In his mind, he took in the next moves of Dodgson and Maber. Brewster Carron was right. The sheepmen had never intended to quit the valley. They were back, and offering a peace plan under the nose of the law. But it was a ruse, a prelude to their roughhousing, the spilled blood of a fight. They'd send hired gunmen across the creeks from the north and south. His small herd would be run into the Pikes to die. The Poll Durhams would probably be taken to a border settlement like Mammoth or Badger Basin and sold for nothing more than a night's gambling money. Those that remained would be shot where they stood, their carcasses left as a brutal message. If *he* was still there, they'd make a move on him, and it wouldn't be just to stove him up.

'I reckon I can put a stop to any o' that happenin',' he asided to Pruett. 'I'm goin' to do what's best for all of us, an' do a little abattoir job on our Mr Dodgson. It's the humane thing to do, an' a town marshal's only got to close his eyes for a moment if he don't agree.'

Pruett swallowed hard. His facial expression veered from amusement to dread as he watched Burt move away from the bar.

Burt didn't even look in the direction of Dodgson as he left the saloon. On the sidewalk, he squinted at the still-rising sun and took a few deep breaths, decided he wasn't going to try and make it back home that day.

He spent the next few hours in his room, resting up some more. It was approaching dusk when he went along to see Hester Brax. She was pleased to see him, and invited him out to the house for supper.

At sun-up the next morning, taking the roan into a fast clip, he left Clayburn for Wild Meddow.

17

The moment Burt rode in, Pitt had a message for him. 'Mr Carron wants us. He's sent a rider,' he called out excitedly. 'The goddamn sheep are back. They're strung along the Pikes ... pressin' hard against Ankle Iron. The boss figures they could be gettin' ready to make a move on him. He said you'd understand.'

'Yeah, I do,' Burt sighed. 'It's his notion of all for one, an' one for all, eh?'

'No, it ain't like that,' Macey said. 'We sent word back. Said that you'd be needin' us ... why you'd gone to Clayburn.'

Burt thanked them for their watchfulness, for feeding his dogs. He knew it didn't matter much whether they stayed or not. If Wild Meddow was indiscriminately attacked, two or three of them weren't going to hold out against a dozen armed sheepherders. Even a tinhorn gambler couldn't raise odds against them being shot dead.

Pitt and Macey tied in their horse strings and set off to Ankle Iron. For what was left of the day, Burt gave preoccupied attention to his dog pack.

Knowing he'd be away from the ranch house, Burt wanted the animals trained to stay around. The pups were already independent for some of the time. They had the full run of the house, the yard and open ground out to the barn. That night, at sundown, Samson accompanied him for a check around the corral and ruined outbuildings; for the most part, he was content to run at heel.

A couple of hours into full dark, Burt got a blanket and some extra cartridges. He saddled a rimrock mare, and rode to the rising ground where his family were buried. In the bright moonlight, from beneath the blue beech he could see most of the way to the south fork of Gray Bull Creek, the sooty specks that were his small herd.

Until the early hours he remained in the saddle, then he dismounted and sat enfolded in his blanket, waiting for first light. But nothing happened. It was the following night when the riders came.

They came off the Pikes during the daylight hours, hid in the creek timber until near midnight, when the moon dropped below the Springfield Hogback. The dull sound of a gunshot echoed along the creek from where two men rode at his herd, and it brought Burt to his feet.

They fired two, then three more shots, as the cattle started their run towards the shelter of the willow brakes. Burt tugged at the mare's cinch and mounted. 'Payback time, Pa,' he rasped. 'Let's give 'em hell.'

Because of the distance from the Wild Meddow ranch house, the riders thought they'd be out of harm's way for an hour or so, and they moved around carelessly. They were even hooting as they switched their attention from six dead heifers to the section that continued to stampede for cover.

Burt heeled his horse into a run, took it fast down the rising slope and on to the range. He swung in an easterly arc to where the north and south forks of the creek connected. He gained on the riders, wanted to trap them in the western end of his land, cut them off from the crossing.

The two men had stopped now. They were wondering which of the breaking groups of heifers to go for when they heard the pounding approach of Burt's mare. Unsuspecting, they hesitated and, under the bright starlight, turned in their saddles. But it was already too late by the time they realized it wasn't a friendly rider from the sheep camp.

Burt pulled the mare into a tight swerve and skidded to a halt. He pulled his carbine and went to ground, took up a kneeling position.

The men ahead of him began firing in fearful and heedless panic. But Burt was too far away for their Colts, and his first big .45 bullet took one of them in the middle of his back when he turned to flee. The featureless figure jerked back then staggered forward before windmilling lifelessly to the ground. The

109

man's horse sank to one side, then sprung its legs and bucked in tenor. The second rider yelled curses and decided to run for the sandy steeps below the Springfield Hogback. It was west, where the bleached, sheep bones lay.

'A fitting end, but you'll never make it,' Burt, hissed icily.

As the man rowelled his horse, he twisted in the saddle, looked back to see if Burt was chasing.

With a tight, twisted grin, Burt took aim again and shot the man high in the right side of his chest. He lowered the rifle, watched as the man clutched with one hand at the mane of his horse. Then he got to his feet, calmly shoved the rifle back into its saddle holster, and swung into the saddle. He gently heeled the mare forward. 'We'll walk . . . a tad more'n he's doin',' he murmured.

Burt kept his eyes alert as he drew close. The man had managed to recover his reins but it was as much as he could do to stay upright. He didn't even turn to confront Burt, who pulled off to one side before swinging the mare in close.

'I got one o' your bullets in me, mister,' the man croaked. 'Goin' to give me another?'

Burt drew his carbine, leaned over and slammed its barrel hard into the man's kneecap. 'Too good for you, maggot breath. You've killed my cattle, an' tried to shoot me dead. So, I'm wonderin' if you smell like roastin' mutton when you got a brandin' iron laid to your ass.'

The man let out a low groan at the agony of his cracked kneecap. 'For chris'sakes, I ain't no lamb licker,' he whined. 'I just took me some work at fightin' wages. You know how it is.'

'Yeah. Tough if you ain't on the winnin' side. Any more o' you fightin' workers on my range this night?' Burt demanded.

'Not that I know of.'

'Who sent you?'

'Texas Smollet. He said you wouldn't have a guard out yet. You weren't supposed to be coverin' the range.'

'I ain't. I'm coverin' my *stock*. What do you know about Smollet?' Burt asked.

'Nothin'. We ain't paid to know about who's payin' us.'

Burt raised the barrel of the rifle threateningly. 'I'd think real hard about that answer, if I was you,' he threatened.

'He's said he wants you under his feet. That's it. I don't know any more.'

Burt's eyes narrowed. 'Do you know where he's from?'

The man shook his head miserably. 'North, maybe.'

Burt guessed the man didn't have much more to offer. 'If that's right, I think Smollet an' me must've had a run-in before. I'm guessin' he knows better'n I do.'

The man gave a raw, almost inaudible grunt.

'That's between you two. You can let me ride, if you ain't goin' to finish me off,' he risked.

Burt nodded in agreement. 'The Canadian border's more'n three hundred miles due north. See how far you can get,' he said.

'I got to get this knee seen to. I'll go by way o' Clayburn.'

Slowly, and with menace, Burt shook his head. 'Canada,' he repeated. 'If you ever make it, get work as a storekeep.' He moved the mare back a few steps, indicated the way north with the tip of his rifle.

Burt speculated that if, when he got to the ridge, the man forked off to warn the sheepmen, it would be late the next day before they returned. He watched the man and his horse walk away, until they vanished into the darkness, then he rode back to where he'd shot the other man. He gathered up the horse that hadn't wandered far and, sweating with the hurt, he managed to rope the man and drag his body up and over the animal's back. He hog-tied the man's feet tight beneath the horse's belly and punched its thigh, sent it trotting towards the north creek crossing. He wanted the body back in Clayburn, off his Wild Meddow range.

18

At the offices of the *Clayburn Tidings*, Grif Pruett walked in from the blistering heat of mid afternoon. He removed his hat, and wiped a bandana across the top of his oily forehead. Fraser Brax greeted him, and Hester smiled from where she was copy-writing at her father's desk.

'Must be hotter'n yesterday,' the marshal suggested.

'Yeah, must be,' Brax answered, rolling his eyes. 'Any more news on the backshot feller?'

'Not yet. There's a whole bunch o' sheepmen in town, an' they don't know anythin' either.'

'Huh, I wonder why that don't surprise me?' Brax said, making a wry smile.

'The rider who brought him in still maintains they was bushwhacked by Burton Lane.'

Hester shook her head despondently. 'Well, *that* must surprise you,' she said, looking to her father.

'What do the sheepmen want?' Brax asked Pruett.

'Right now, they're loadin' up with supplies.'

'You goin' to do anythin' about it?'

Pruett gave Brax a quizzical look. 'Buyin' flour an' beans from Pinch Cutler's peaceable enough,' he said. 'Can you see a problem in that, Fraser?'

'I'm goin' to in about ten minutes,' Brax nodded that he could. 'I just seen Jethro an' Jake with their boys. Looked to me like they were headed straight for trouble.'

'Yeah, I saw that. I warned 'em off, too,' Pruett said. 'We ain't buildin' much of a story there, I'm afraid.'

But both men had got it wrong.

'Hell!' Pruet yelled, and they ran from the building as the first blast of gunfire exploded along the street.

A bunch of Single Rig men ran from the doors of the Fallen Drummer. They were shooting back into the building as they jumped to the street.

Pruett cursed. 'They're Poole's waddies,' he yelled this time as he started off along the sidewalk.

Brax was close behind as the marshal pushed his way through the batwings. Jake and Jethro Poole were standing with their backs to the bar. On their left, two of their ranch hands were watching a corner table.

Vaughn Maber and Texas Smollet were sitting with their own hired men, one of whom had taken a bullet across the flesh of his neck. Another man glanced warily at the marshal, as he dabbed his

114

colleague's bloody wound with whiskey.

Pruett halted in the center of the floor, and Brax backed up to the bar to assess the story.

'Well, you wouldn't want to *drink* that rotgut',' Pruett rasped. 'Now all o' you get out, an' take the walkin' wounded with you,' he commanded.

Not one of the men appeared to move, and Pruett turned his attention to Jethro Poole.

'You got a short memory, Jethro? I just got through tellin' you not to cause any trouble. What the hell is it with you cowmen?'

'You stay out o' this, Grif. We're tellin' these lamb lickers they don't belong, in language they understand. Hah, we got ourselves a sort o' quarantine.'

'Quarantine?' Pruett sneered. 'Why, a blow fly's higher in the social order than some o' the folk you're mixin' with, Jethro. How the hell did this start?'

'What difference does that make?' Maber interjected.

'We told 'em to leave, but this one here went for his gun,' Jake said indicating the man he'd shot. 'I was just showin' him the error of his ways. Anyhow, it weren't nothin' more'n self-defence, Marshal.'

'That's as maybe, but what did your boys need to shoot the place up for,' Pruett enquired testily.

'Ah, they just got a tad excited. It weren't nothin' more.'

Pruett took a deep breath, momentarily closed his

eyes with frustration. 'I've decided your wagon's loaded,' he told Maber. 'An' before anythin' else happens, I'm orderin' you to get out o' town.' To emphasize his command, the marshal drew his Colt. He moved it in a way that suggested the sheepmen get out of their chairs and follow him.

The men assembled on the sidewalk outside of the saloon, watched amazed as a heavily loaded wagon raced along the street towards them. The driving seat was empty, but a Single Rig cowboy was riding alongside, holding the reins of the mule team.

'What the sweet jumpin'—' was one man's reaction as the rider dragged the team into a straight line.

The mules were bog-eyed with panic, and the big wagon swayed drunkenly. Some of the trace chains had been unhooked and, laden with food supplies, the whole outfit was headed for a break-up. A mixed bunch of riders from the valley ranches chased up close behind. They were hollering, waving their hats with one hand, firing of their guns in the other.

'They must o' tanked my mules up on locoweed to make 'em run like that,' Maber rasped, while the Poole brothers shrugged insolently.

The dust from beneath the wheels almost hid the wagon as it careered to the very edge of town. Then the cowboy let the team free and, snapping the remaining traces, the mules ran on wildly. The wagon swerved and hit the base of a half-empty water tower. With a grinding of wood and iron, it heeled and twisted over on to its side. Through the choking alkali clouds, most of the sheepmen's provisions were strewed wretchedly across the hard-packed dirt.

Pruett stepped down from the sidewalk. 'Jethro, you an' Jake stand aside,' he told the Poole brothers 'The first man to pull a gun gets correctional facilities for a week.'

Jethro considered a response as he looked to his brother, then nodded his observance. 'You heard the marshal,' he called out reluctantly. 'Let 'em go. They won't be botherin' us again today.'

The sheepmen who'd been watching stepped uneasily from different buildings along the street. Maber and Smollet strolled grudgingly to where all the horses were hitched. The injured man threw a mean look back at Jake, but he saw the marshal was watching him, and changed his mind about going for his gun.

Pruett turned stiffly as one of Pinch Cutler's store clerks came running up.

'They ain't paid,' the man flustered. 'They owe me for the supplies.'

'Yeah, sometimes life's a real haul,' Pruett drawled irritatedly. 'You go an' tell Pinch that if he wants payment, Vaughn Maber's still in town. But then, so's the supplies, by the look of it. Unless you want to sift sand an' flour, I'd think about chalkin' it up.'

What Vaughn Maber had in mind though, came quick, and it wasn't anything like what Marshal Pruett had in mind. Slanted across the street, the

117

man roughly kicked his horse into movement. Having already pulled his Colt on the blind side, Maber twisted in the saddle, fired off three quick shots at the group of men who were standing outside of the saloon.

As Jake Poole's Colt cleared leather, Jethro made a grab for his brother's wrist. But Maber was wild with anger, and by the time his wayward bullets had crashed into the low clapboards of the Fallen Drummer, all the sheepmen were away. They had their heads down, were headed for out of town and the open range.

Pruett was standing his ground, had hardly moved. His mind raced at the implications of what had just happened, what it would mean. Without their essential supplies, the sheepmen would have to make another arrangement, and soon. Someone was going to pay, and from where Pruett stood, it looked like Fraser Brax could be right about the settlers along Gray Bull Creek.

Meantime, he'd look at the circulars sent out from the county seat. He thought there might be some word on the dead man who rode into town, hog-tied to his horse.

19

It wasn't long after midday when Burt heard Delia growl from beyond the barn. And from somewhere out near the sheds, Samson gave a low, threatening bark. Burt grabbed his carbine, quickly moved to the half-open door.

The dogs barked in unison as the threat got closer, as the lone rider emerged from the creekside timber and headed directly for the ranch.

Cradling the rifle, Burt took a step on to the belt of ground that had been cleared to the home pasture. 'Samson . . . Delia!' he shouted, and the dogs stopped their warning noises. They were still bristling and wary, but walked at heel as Burt walked out to meet Hester Brax.

Burt raised his hand in greeting. 'They ain't too sure yet the difference 'tween friend an' foe,' he called out as she drew close.

'I hope that doesn't include eatin' a messenger,' Hester replied.

'Messenger? This ain't a social visit?'

'Yes it is, Burt. But what I got to tell you's made it sooner rather than later.'

'What's that, Hester?'

'Grif Pruett's got a warrant for your arrest.'

'My arrest! What for? Who from?'

'You're supposed to have murdered someone. It's from the man who brought in the body.'

'Ah, him . . . the lucky one,' Burt said, reaching out to take hold of the bay's cheek strap. 'Did he need some help in gettin' out o' the saddle . . . carry a bullet wound near his right arm pit?'

'Yes, he did. Was it you shot him?'

'Yeah. I took exception to them killin' my cattle. What was *his* story?'

'He said they were lookin' for work, but someone ambushed them south o' Gray Bull Creek.'

Sudden anger gripped Burt's insides. The man he'd let ride north *had* turned back after all. If the pair of them had no links with the sheepmen, they probably *would* have passed as itinerant ranch hands. 'I'm still learnin' somethin' from sheepmen,' he said, through the grind of teeth. 'Forgivin' *don't* always end a quarrel. No matter what they tell you at Sunday School.'

Hester saw the turmoil in Burt's face. 'I'm sorry,' she said. 'I told Pa, I didn't believe it.'

'Well, that's somethin',' he replied. 'I been called many things, but never a bushwhacker. There'll be time for you to eat before you return,' he then suggested shyly. 'I ain't that far from bein' civilized. Although I don't recall bein' called it much.'

'So, we'll see,' Hester said with an agreeable smile as she climbed down from her horse. She'd seen the bulldog pups as they tumbled from around the corner of the corral fence. She went to kneel beside them, but drew away when they both yipped and gnashed their teeth.

'Sorry, they ain't a playful breed,' Burt quickly explained. 'They're bein' brought up as guard dogs.'

Hester stood back. She eyed the young dogs uneasily while Burt collected his roan and walked it back to the barn to saddle up. Minutes later, Burt led the way through the home pasture and up the rising grassy trail, north of the ranch house.

'I didn't think you'd mind ridin' up this way,' he said, half an hour later, where they stopped beneath the shady overhang of the blue beeches.

'No, that's alright,' she said, looking down at the gravestones of Burt's family.

'You can see the span o' the land from here . . . some o' the best grazin'.' Burt pointed to the east, along the creekside willow. 'You can even see the carcasses o' my dead heifers,' he added harshly. 'Those that fell with gunhands' bullets in 'em.'

Burt turned silent as he swung his horse south, down towards the creek. After an absorbed moment, Hester followed.

'Is there a way out o' this mess?' she spoke up, as they approached the creekside willows.

'Oh, there sure as hell *is*, young lady,' Texas Smollet called out, as he moved his horse from cover of the timber.

Burt cursed, groaned in desperation. Out of the corner of an eye, he saw Smollet and two riders close behind him. Knowing this time he'd die unless he acted fast, he cursed again. It wasn't likely that him and Smollet had one single thing in common, except that neither of them were up for another chance.

Burt was already moving as his thoughts got real. He leaped from the saddle, towards Hester. Wanting to jump them away from where he knew the bullets would come, he yelled, and punched a fist into the bay's rump. Then he went to ground, turned on to his back and pulled his Colt. The bullets were already breaking up the ground beside him as he shot one of the men behind Smollet. The man gurgled bloodily, threw up both hands to claw at his shattered throat, as he fell from the saddle. Surrounded by the crash of guns, the riderless horse screamed in terror, lashed out its forelegs at the rear of Smollet's mount.

Smollet tried to gain control of his mount, and Burt couldn't find him with a bullet. The man realized the ferocity of Burt's pent-up emotions was making up for any disadvantage. The harsh, choking cries of his colleague on the ground panicked him into turning his horse back towards the creek.

Burt heard Hester cry out as he fired off more offensive rounds, but there was no time to look out for her. He curled up and started to reload his Colt, jerked involuntarily as bullets got closer to his body. Using his elbows, he dragged himself to where earth runnels met the broken ground of the creek timber. The second of Smollet's back-up riders was bearing down on him, but it was Texas Smollet that Burt wanted. He fired into the willows, but knew he was wasting bullets. Already Smollet would be spurring his horse along the creek, heading towards the sandy steeps of the Springfield Hogback.

The back-up rider had halted his run, was suddenly shooting wildly. He was fearful of Burt and called out for Smollet's help. Burt shot him high in the leg, and he swayed in the saddle. His horse felt the loss of control and went into a frightened gallop, away from the sound of the gunfire.

Burt went into a crouching run. He reached the creek, pressed his back against the bole of a willow. A bullet chewed into the silvery bark alongside his head and he cursed and ducked. The man on the ground had been mortally wounded, though, and had fired his last shot. He was dead before Burt hit him again.

In frustration, Burt fired another bullet along the creek. He stepped calmly into the open, then, as a signal of his endurance, sent a final shot into the air. On instinct, he looked far out to the west, caught sight of a rider who'd quickly moved in and out of the timber. He loaded up again, looked pensively around him, and pushed the Colt back into its holster.

20

Hester's face was drained of color, and she was carrying the reins of Burt's horse. As she approached, he met her with a sombre look.

'Hah, accordin' to Warner Herrick, that was just badgerin',' he said drily. 'Let's hope we're not around if an' when they got their scuts up.' He ignored the body on the ground, waved a hand at the loose horse to run it off.

'Who were they?' Hester asked quietly.

'A man called Texas Smollet, an' two of his pack. I think he's been here before, but that was a long time past, and he had the Plummers' sheep outfit with him then.'

'Was he one of the men who murdered your family?'

Burt nodded sharply. 'Yeah, but they ain't rightly *men*, Hester. They're *sheepmen*, an' there's a big difference. I think Smollet's the reason Dodgson and Maber tried to muscle in on Wild Meddow. I think he'd convinced 'em they could get in here, despite the cost.'

Hester handed Burt his reins. 'I was goin' to say I understand, but I don't think I do, really. But it has reminded me what else I was goin' to tell you. Some of those sheepmen raided a farm along the creek . . . took some food supplies an' a horse. There's goin' to be a farmers' meetin' tonight. Pa's advisin' them to get organized to protect themselves.'

Burt nodded in consideration. 'Yeah, why not?' he said. 'Well, you an' me's already had an eventful day, an' I'm sorry for it. You should be leavin' right away, I guess.'

'I'm not goin' anywhere, just yet. The trails are too dangerous. I might run into those men. If it's all right with you, I'll stay over, get an early start in the morning.'

Burt smiled, immediately wondered who would believe that that was Hester's suggestion. 'Well, I reckon you'd be safe enough, but then again, you've probably heard that I've got me a bakin' oven. How about canned peach pie?' he suggested.

'What with?'

'Beans an' gravy,' he laughed, climbing into the saddle. 'Let's go eat.'

Later, Burt made coffee and called for Samson. 'I haven't slept inside the house too much recently, besides, I stay awake most nights. There're shouldn't be any more fightin', but I'll take this rascal an' have a scout around.'

As Burt hesitated in the doorway, Hester left the table and stepped up to him. She stood very close and lifted her face. Burt held her shoulders, gave her a short but important kiss. Then he smiled, grabbed his rifle and walked into the starlit night. With the way things were stacking up, there was no way he was going to scout around his ranch. He nestled among the grain sacks, slept alongside the muscular comfort of Samson.

He was awake before the sun broke from the distant Bighorns. Hester had already made warm scones, and the coffee pot sat atop the stove. After the early breakfast, he saddled their horses and accompanied her to the crossing at the north fork of Gray Bull Creek.

'At the first sign o' trouble, take your hat off, an' tumble your tresses. Let 'em see you're just a slip of a lass,' he advised.

'Hmm, an' hope we don't get to the second sign,' she said with a nervous smile.

Ruse Barrow was sitting on the planked stoop, waiting, when Burt got back.

'I guess you been too busy enjoyin' yourself to have heard the news,' he said, getting to his feet, extending his big hand in greeting.

Burt realized that it must have been Barrow who'd rode from the timber along the south creek, and that the farmer must have seen him with Hester. 'How'd you mean?' he answered uneasily, not wanting to give much away.

'Hah, you haven't heard, have you? Our little stock war's over.'

Burt stopped from turning the key in the door lock, turned slowly to look at Barrow.

'The sheepmen have trailed through the Pikes, gone south,' Barrow continued. 'They reckon there's enough land down there for summer an' winter grazin'. That's the word from Clover City. Warner Herrick's confirmed it.'

'Well, we'll know which way to send the wolves then,' Burt mumbled. He listened with deep scepticism as Barrow told him that Herrick had been in Clayburn the day before. The sheriff had been telling all who'd listen that the sheepmen were giving up their land push, Wild Meddow included.

'Come in, and have some coffee. It's still hot. I got me a stove,' Burt said distractedly.

Barrow stayed talking for fifteen minutes. He didn't mention that there was a warrant of any kind out for Burt, and Burt didn't ask.

When the farmer had gone, Burt did some thinking. He couldn't believe the sheepmen had quit. It wasn't their way. What they wanted, they took, or died trying. But if it *was* the truth, there was something else. Like the personal vengeance of Texas Smollet. Yeah, that was more likely to be it. There would be no more waiting, though. What was it that his father had said? If the fight's inescapable, get in first, take it to them and don't compromise, *ever.* So Burt went to the barn and saddled up the roan, packed two boxes of .45 cartridges into the saddle-bags.

It was a sharp, crystal-clear night, when Burt nudged his horse along Clayburn's main street. He intended to be very circumspect until he found out what the law intended to do about serving the warrant.

The door to the newspaper offices was open, and Burt tied the roan to the hitching rail outside. He stepped up on to the sidewalk, could see there was no sign of Hester, just Fraser Brax working at his desk.

As Burt stepped through the door, Brax turned.

'Evenin',' he said. 'You must've heard the excitement's over. Over before it's started, you could say.'

'You *could*,' Burt replied. 'But then you wouldn't have much of a lead story. *I'd* say it wasn't, 'cause I don't think it *is.*'

Brax jabbed his ink pen back in its pot. 'So why have Dodgson and Maber pulled their sheep to the Needle foothills.'

'Ask the cattlemen who were out wavin' 'em goodbye,' Burt smiled his derision. 'A warm, kindly send-off with Yearlin' Timms an' the Poole brothers.'

Brax quickly nodded. 'Yeah, maybe. I did suggest the farmers get 'emselves armed ... throw up some sort of resistance. Do you think that's blowin' in the wind?' he said, seeing that Burt wasn't too encouraged.

128

'Yeah, somethin' like that. I think Texas Smollet's convinced Dodgson an' Maber to take in Wild Meddow as they push up through the creeks. That's why I'm here in town,' Burt responded grimly.

'Hester told me what happened,' Brax said. 'Not all of it, I suspect, but you'd o' guessed that.'

'Yeah, she is your daughter. She also told me of the murder warrant.'

Brax shook his head slowly, rubbed his eyes. 'I doubt much will come o' that. Grif Pruett ain't about to take the word of someone who's wanted for robbin' just about every bank west o' the Bighorn.'

'So where does that leave me?'

'As you were, I suppose,' Brax said, getting to his feet. 'I'll find out. Get yourself over to the house an' see that daughter o' mine. I'll meet you back here in an hour.'

When Burt had gone, Brax tidied up his desk before grabbing his hat and coat. He locked the door of the office and strolled along to Lefty Detes to find the town marshal.

21

Burt knew there was only one person who Brax could have asked about the warrant, and he went to find him.

Grif Pruett was in the saloon. He was at the bar, talking with some of the more important cattlemen.

Burt nodded at the group. 'Did Mr Brax come in to see you?' he asked of the marshal.

'Yep, he did. An' now he's gone home.'

'No he ain't,' Burt said. 'An' I don't think he intended to go there either. That's odd, 'cause he told me Hester would be there, an' the place is in darkness.'

'Well, that's where he said he was goin'. You must've missed him.'

'Hmm, not likely,' Burt muttered uncertainly. 'What did he want to talk to you about?' he asked, still wondering about Hester.

'You. An' it sounded like ol' Fraser was real

concerned about your health.'

Both men were thoughtful for a moment, and before either of them said any more, Jethro Poole spoke up.

'It could be that you ain't plannin' to poke your head through a noose any more,' he said, cheerfully.

Behind Poole, his brother Jake was standing with Brewster Carron. 'For whatever reason, it looks like just about everybody's hit town tonight,' Carron observed.

Burt didn't want to get too involved. He wanted to get on with what he had to do. But Jake Poole was thinking otherwise, held up his hand as a restraining gesture.

'Hey, feller, I reckon we're all deservin' of a drink,' he said. 'It'll be a cold night in hell before we catch sight o' them bleat monkeys again.'

Burt gave the men a long, speculative look. 'I've known that kind since I was knee-high,' he said. 'Like I been tellin' one o' the creek farmers, they ain't *gone*. They're *somewhere*.'

Burt was about to continue with his suspicions, when Fraser Brax entered the saloon. The man was wide-eyed, as he slammed the batwings aside.

'Hester's gone,' he said, reeling towards the bar. And then to Burt, 'I said for you to call on her. Did you see her . . . anythin'? Have *they* got to her? Where the hell is she?'

Burt shook his head. 'I don't know. I didn't see her,' he responded quickly. 'You said she was there, but I didn't make much of it, 'cause she weren't expectin' me. Who's they? Are you talkin' about the sheepmen?'

'Yeah, who else? They broke in through the back . . . busted the door open.'

The cattlemen gave each other troubled looks and exchanged a few incredulous curses.

'I saw Smollet earlier. It was at the back end o' town,' Carron said. 'Looked like he'd been at the gut warmer. Huh, some of his own sheep dip, more'n likely.'

Brax smiled weakly, then swallowed a whiskey that Jake had set in front of him. 'Hester's bay was still in the shed stall,' he said, and coughed.

'If it *was* them, they'd o' brought in a spare horse,' Burt suggested. He felt the dull hurt of his wound and got to thinking of the man who was responsible, the man he was setting out to look for.

'If it's ransom they're after, they've drawn the short straw with you, Fraser. With respect,' Pruett suggested to Brax.

'Yeah, it don't make sense,' Brax retorted.

'It does to me,' Burt said. 'Smollet knows what he's doin'.' Burt now knew why for some time Smollet and his men had been tagging him. They were seeking a weakness, and they'd found it. 'It is the sheepmen and they've taken her out to Wild Meddow. That's what they'll be wantin' to trade her for,' he explained briefly.

Although it was his own daughter in trouble, Brax

132

saw Burt's resolve, and thought it best to accept the defiant man's proposal.

'What's to stop 'em killin' you, the minute you sign them documents?' Marshal Pruett chipped in.

'Nothin', I guess. My sole intention's to see Hester safe an' away from there. It ain't up for debate, an' I'm goin' alone.'

Brewster Carron nodded gravely. 'Every dyin' man's entitled to a last wish, Lane, an' I'll be carryin' out yours,' he said.

'An' what do you reckon that'll be?' Burt asked.

'Within minutes o' the girl bein' safe, we'll kill every goddamn sheepman within fifty miles o' here.'

Burt grinned. 'Make it a hundred. Now I got to see a man about a bullet,' he said, and walked from the bar.

Carron looked around him. 'I want every available man roused. Pull 'em from their bath chairs, if necessary. Make sure they're armed an' saddled an' outside o' here within an hour,' he said forcefully.

Out on the sidewalk, Grif Pruett stood watching a group of men who rode through the pools of thin lamplight. Six of them reined in and dismounted, took note of the aggressive excitement around them. One of them, a big, powerfully built man, nodded politely at the marshal as he led the way up the steps and through the batwings of the saloon.

From the opposite direction, Jethro Poole drew in

his horse as Pruett was about to follow the men inside.

'Who the hell are those guys, Grif?' he called out.

'Don't recognize any o' 'em. But by the look of 'em, they ain't ridin' with sheep. Perhaps they're up to takin' sides,' the marshal pondered.

The newcomers were gathered at the bar. Standing near, looking worried and bleary-eyed, was Fraser Brax. He was talking to Yearling Timms and several cowboys.

Pruett went back in to the saloon, resolutely advanced on the tough-looking men.

'Just tell me you ain't anythin' to do with sheepmen,' he challenged. 'Otherwise I'll be forced to shoot the lot o' you.'

The big man coolly waited until he'd ordered up whiskeys and beers for his men, then he turned and gave Pruett a calculating look. 'Just *thinkin'* sheep's a real serious offence where we come from, Marshal,' he said with a trace of intimidation. 'I'm Noble Rockford, an' this here's Milo Tedder. He's responsible for bringin' Burt Lane's herd down from Musselshell.'

'Rockford, eh,' Pruett said. 'Well, I guess I heard o' you.'

'An' I'm here because I heard that young Burt's got himself spread across a package o' trouble.'

'I hope you ain't referrin' to my daughter,' Brax intervened angrily. 'It's *her* that Lane's gone to fight over. Right this minute, sheep considerations ain't a

134

main concern.'

'What do you mean?' Rockford asked. 'What's your *daughter* got to do with this?'

'Her name's Hester. She's the *ransom* for Wild Meddow, an' it's the goddamn sheepmen who took her.'

Rockford was thinking while he swallowed his beer. 'Principled would be one way o' describin' Burt Lane,' he asserted. 'Principled an' steadfast. So there must be somethin' between him an' your daughter.'

'Yeah, there's somethin'. Newspaper editors ain't proper equipped for gunfightin', or else—' Brax gave up on his wishful threat, banged down another empty glass. 'Burt should be half way out there by now,' he said.

Rockford studied his whiskey chaser. 'If Burt Lane's gone gunnin' for these sheepmen, he won't be doin' it out there, believe me,' he assured Brax and Pruett. 'Me an' my boys will ride for Wild Meddow when we've taken on grub. I'm gettin' me an interest in this territory.'

'Your man's forked over a steamin' heap o' trouble this time,' Tedder said.

'Sure sounds like it,' Rockford agreed. 'But we'll get out there soon enough. At least we know he's got fresh horses, 'cause we know who bred 'em,' he added drily.

Brax suddenly shook himself into looming reality. 'Mr Rockford, there's somethin' else,' he said. 'I think it's got some bearin' on what's happenin' here.

135

I'm sorry but it won't wait until you've taken your food. If you come to the newspaper office, I'll explain on the way.'

22

In the *Clayburn Tidings* office, Brax singled out an envelope from the locked drawer of his desk. He glanced at the writing on the front, then handed it to Rockford.

'It was you bein' here . . . your name, that got me thinkin',' he said. 'I think you should be readin' this. Go ahead an' open it.'

Noble Rockford stood under a hanging lamp. With an deadpan expression, he read the paper, then read it again.

It was written by Burt Lane, and below the date, it said:

In the event of my death, I leave the property known as Wild Meddow to Noble Harper Rockford from Musselshell. This will take in any cattle and livestock. If Mr Rockford decides to reward whoever kills the man or men that kill me with any of that property, I'm not going to argue.
Burton C. Meddow.

'He weren't one for the official line, but he sure managed to spell out his meanin'. An' it's signed by him who wrote it, so it's legal,' Rockford said, handing over Burt's note for Brax to read. 'He must've known I'd be actin' on his behalf.'

Brax refolded the paper and placed it back inside the envelope. 'Yeah, I guess so. Do you know these men he's gone after?' he asked.

'Oh yeah,' Rockford said. 'I feel like I know 'em real well.'

'You ain't got many men with you,' Brax pointed out.

'That handful o' men are a hell of a lot more'n *many*,' Rockford responded sharply. With that, he turned and walked from Brax's office. But he had been affected by the dread and helplessness in the newspaperman's eyes. 'Your daughter's safe enough,' he assured him. 'It's Wild Meddow they want. If they harm her, there'll be *nothin'* left in this world for 'em to enjoy.'

Near to midnight, Cole Dodgson and Vaughn Maber rode ahead of Texas Smollet and Hester Brax. They approached a north bank crossing of Gray Bull Creek, moved slowly now, after a fast run from Clayburn. Occasionally, Maber dropped back to get a close look at Hester who rode ungagged and unbound. She'd lapsed into what the sheepmen took to be a brooding, frightened silence, but under their watchful eyes her mind was racing with thoughts of breaking away.

Dodgson walked his horse into the creek water. 'Vaughn, Tex,' he called, indicated that the two men and Hester ride around him. Then he twisted around in the saddle and called to another group of men who were following close. 'Farrer, you ride on now. When you get there, keep to the open ground, and call for him to come out. Tell him what's been arranged . . . the deal an' the girl.'

A tight, hunched man with a slung bandolier drew his horse alongside Dodgson. 'Suppose he ain't in an accommodatin' mood. Suppose he's standin' off from the house, just watchin'. From what I've heard, this Lane feller ain't no pigeon.'

'Well, he won't shoot you, lame-head. You're the one who's goin' to take him to the girl. If he ain't there, an' you hear nothin', go on into the house and light a lamp. If he *is* watchin', that'll bring him in. I'll be coverin' you when you're back on the trail.'

The man named Farrer sniffed and looked doubtful, heel-kicked his horse through the shallow water. He could just make out the buildings of Wild Meddow that were further to the east, squat and dark in the moonlight.

Dodgson nodded at the two other men, then galloped ahead to the sandy steeps at the base slope of the Springfield Hogback. As he rode, he scanned the darkness ahead until he saw the riders ahead of him.

Maber saw him, pointed out to beyond where they

rode. It was where many years of shrub and weed growth covered the bleached, broken bones of the Lagger sheep.

'Yeah, I know what's there,' Dodgson said tellingly.

The trail the riders were on sided tight to the base of the ridge. The ground was broken shale, left virtually no sign for anyone who might be on their tail. Dodgson knew they'd be coming, and who it would be, felt secure in his choice of bolt hole. 'You know it, Tex. Take 'em on,' he said. 'Get yourselves snugged in. I've got a meetin' with Farrer an' Lane.'

Smollet reined his horse away. He was followed by Maber who was now leading Hester's mount. A quarter of a mile further on, roosting blue jays were disturbed, fluttered from the topmost branches of a stand of Ponderosa pine. Many years before, the trees had pushed from the ground up close to a fault in the ridge. Now, their trunks concealed the deep, sandstone fracture that allowed passage for Smollet, Maber and Hester Brax and their horses. It was a natural void that would keep them hidden away from the trail. Dodgson had learned of it from Smollet. It was secure and well defendable shelter if he had to hold the girl.

On the south fork of the creek, at the edge of the willow stand, Burt was sitting his roan. He was deep in thought as Samson and Delia's barking fractured the night air.

Charging down the house would be a wrong thing

to do. As a witness, Hester was already a dangerous liability to the sheepmen. But for the moment, Burt knew she would come to no harm. She was the trade goods they needed for the deal. They were both safe up until the moment he signed his name. But later, she'd be expendable, in as much danger as himself. It was a deadly game, and he had to play it right.

He dismounted, ground-hitched the roan, and stamped his feet to get circulation moving. With his eyes aching to see in the darkness, he looked again towards the house, cursed softly when he saw the swing of a lantern in the distance. The yellow light beckoned, but he wasn't falling for it. It wasn't from a window, unless someone had unshuttered them.

The nerve at the corner of Burt's eye flickered and he grinned unkindly. Someone had unwittingly let the dogs out of their shed, so they would have given anyone trying to enter his house a hard time. In and around the outbuildings, their sounds were definitely moving around fast. Burt didn't know if there'd be more than one man up there, guessed there might be if they wanted to make certain of nabbing him.

There'd been no barking for a few minutes, and Burt decided it was time he made a move. Keeping low, he went forward, knew Samson and Delia's attention would be diverted, that they'd sense it was *him* out there.

They did, and when he was half way to the house, they were on him. 'Hey, ease up,' he said, as from six

141

feet, both dogs leapt at him, chest high. 'An' keep quiet. You want us all dead?'

Samson grunted his irritation at not being able to go with the excitement, but both the dogs obeyed him. 'Sit down,' Burt commanded. 'Stay until I come back.'

Wide-circling the corral and his stock horses, Burt approached the barn. From the cover of a stack of sawn timber, he could see the front and side of the house. He stood unmoving in the silence, couldn't hear a thing, not even the sounds of any tethered saddle horses. But they were there, he could feel their alien closeness on his land. He realized they were probably in the house by now, made their way in when the dogs had run off. Maybe they were waiting for him, occupying his twin chairs, feet up on his blanket chest.

He pulled his Colt and walked determinedly to the narrow rear door. 'If I'm not here to call 'em off, my dogs'll do more'n eat you. Yeah, harm one hair o' *my* head an' they'll tear you limb from limb,' he felt like calling out. He tried the doorhandle, recalled it was a fresh-greased movement, as the door slide inward, away from him. The scullery was empty, but he could smell the fresh bite of lamp oil as he stepped in. Then another thought crossed his mind. Why was there no sound? Why should they be so quiet, if they didn't know he was there? He stepped into his bedroom, immediately felt the coolness of the night, saw the lower half of his window had been raised and left open. 'Hell, they've been an' gone,' he said out loud. Cursing, Burt ran back through the house. He rushed headlong past the barn and the dog shed, where he guessed the pups were safely hushed in sleep. Towards the creek, Samson and Delia had raised themselves, were into swerving runs, excited again as they all ran for the ground-hitched roan. It was only then that Burt heard the sound of the riders. He went to ground, pulled the dogs in around him. He lay on his back, stared up at the sky. He wanted to listen and get a feel for his predicament, to think, to create the advantage of an edge.

In the flat, gray darkness before dawn, Burt rolled over to see the bunch of riders milling around the house and yard.

'Lane. You in there?' Jethro Poole's voice rose above the general clamor.

'He ain't nowhere around. Let's ride,' an impatient voice shouted back.

Burt hissed out the breath he'd been holding in. It wasn't the sheepmen or their hired gunnies. It was the cowboys hoping for something to break, and he should have known they weren't going to leave him to do battle alone. Hester's abduction would have triggered their assault. And across the valley there'd be others charged up to help now, of that he was absolutely certain. But that would complicate the situation, might even wreck the deal.

Burt watched while the men dismounted, saw them turn their horses into the corral. He had a long look around him, and decided to make a run for his roan at the creekside willow. He pointed to the ranch house. 'Your pups will be up an' hungry. Now get yourselves goin',' he ordered the dogs.

23

Burt rode west to the Springfield Hogback. He knew the sheepmen would pull back when they discovered the rumpus they'd created. He gave them that much sense. But it meant he couldn't make a fast deal for Hester, wherever she was. There weren't many places to hide out in, only the ridge and its old trails and hidey-places that Burt had known from years back.

A half hour later, he turned south along the shale, moved cautiously on from where the overgrown track led to the high, pine-topped rim. Keeping his eye on the broken walls of the ridge, he stayed east of the sandy steeps and the sheep bones. He was in little doubt that he was close to where his quarry was staked out.

Burt unsaddled the roan, and removed its bridle. 'Now it's *your* turn to go home,' he said. He pulled his carbine from its scabbard and slapped the horse's rump. 'If there's anyone left, tell 'em I may be late for supper.'

Watching his footfalls, careful not to send too much shale sliding to the track below, Burt climbed diagonally up to an outcrop. With his back against the wall, he hunkered down on the spur. He laid the rifle beside him, pulled at the brim of his hat and waited quietly.

There was no sound, only the slightest of movements below him. Burt squinted, saw the speckly flash of a ground bird as it scuttled across the rough track. Something or somebody had disturbed it from its home in the fault. It was what Burt knew to be the only stand of timber along the old track. 'Goddamn roadrunner,' he muttered. 'Probably had itself a little ol' caterpillar ranch under the trees.'

Burt inched his way back down to the trail. 'Smollet knows o' this place, goddamnit,' he swore with frustration. He looked up at the topmost branches that spread darkly across the ridge trail and he cursed again. He knew there was no other way into the fault, and he couldn't drop in unexpected from above. If they caught him there in the open, he'd be the fairground target, so he'd have to edge his way forward through the pines.

As he got closer, he realized that the advantage was actually swinging his way. Sure they'd see *him* at the same time he saw *them*, but *he* knew it and was ready. Focusing on what lay about the deeply ribbed bark of the Ponderosas, he levelled the barrel of the carbine.

Without warning, the re-settled jays protested their way up from the branches again. Burt knew that any lookout would have taken note of that disturbance, and he flinched into a frozen silence. Then he countered their thinking, and went forward instead of impulsively shrinking back. He eased the carbine through the timber, worked his way into, and then through the fault until he could see the sandstone floor ahead of him.

There was no sudden confrontation or blast of gunfire, and less than thirty feet away he saw Hester. She had a blanket draped around her shoulders, her back against the slope of a low sandy drift. As far as he could tell, she was unharmed and not restrained in any way.

Vaughn Maber and Texas Smollet were partly hidden by a vertical slab in one of the inner ridge walls. It sounded to Burt as though they'd been having a disagreement, was probably why they hadn't noticed the anxious flight of the jays.

'Cole said we should o' been gone from here, after sun-up,' Smollet complained. 'Well it's sure after that *now*.'

'We ain't got anywhere else to be,' Maber said, his voice gruff and edgy. 'Maybe there's been a mix-up.'

'That's what gets men into boot hill.' There was a sound of creeping unease from Smollet.

'Ah, can it, Tex,' Maber went on. 'They'll be here, an' we're safe enough.'

'Yeah, well it's just *who's* gettin' here that worries

147

me. Territory folk ain't goin' to ignore the kidnappin' of a newspaperman's daughter.'

'There's somethin' else that's got you rattled,' Maber said and gave a low laugh.

'That's right, there *is*,' Smollet agreed. 'You know what they say about history repeatin' itself? Well, there's some at the back of all this. I heard Ike Plummer was lucky to escape with his bits in all the right places.'

'Yeah well, that's the nature o' this business, but escape we do,' Maber snorted. 'But right now we're as safe as a den full o' snufflin' cubs.'

Smollet looked towards Hester. 'An' you reckon Lane's goin' to give his land away in return for the girl?'

'Hah, he ain't exactly givin' it away,' Maber said, lowering his voice. 'Take a good look at her, Tex. Cole reckons she's flower enough for Lane to get himself killed.'

'Huh, Cole says *this*, Cole reckons *that*,' Smollet rasped. 'That young madam's probably goin' to put us all behind bars.'

'Yeah? How the hell's she goin' to do that?' Maber asked after a moment's thought.

'Well, on a hunch, I'd say if Cole don't get rid of her after the deal, she might just be snorty enough to see us all in court. Remember, she has seen an' hear everythin'.'

Maber turned to take a sharp look at Hester. 'You don't think—' he started, but checked his thoughts

148

the moment Burt stepped into the open.

'She ain't goin' to be mad at you two,' Burt said harshly and levered the carbine's trigger guard. 'You're both long dead.'

'Lane,' Texas Smollet recognized the voice, snarled in grave defeat. He dragged wildly at his holster as he twisted to face Burt. But he didn't get to fire his gun. He managed to raise his hand, but that was all.

'You had too many chances, Smollet,' Burt rasped, as he fired a bullet into the man's chest. 'You ain't ever gettin' another,' he added, and fired again as Smollet's body hit the ground.

Vaughn Maber's shots were missing, exploding and splintering the pine stand behind Burt. 'Where the hell are they?' he gasped. 'Farrer . . . Dodgson?'

Burt took a step back, thought of Hester who still hadn't made a move. But she had seen the demonstration of Burt's long-held anger, and it was too late for him to look like a man with leniency on his mind.

As Maber strutted forward, his face dark and thunderous with rage, Burt shot into the ground between them. He thought he could somehow stop the man's advance, but it was no more than a futile gesture. 'So go an' join Smollet,' he said, and lifted the carbine to fire point blank. Shattered by the blast, Maber's legs buckled and he crumpled lifeless at Burt's feet. Burt levered up another round and thought about pulling the trigger one more time.

But that was it. A few seconds of madly reverberating noise, the acrid bite from a curl of cordite smoke, and it was over.

'I wonder how your pa would've covered this quarrel?' he said with a bitter edge to his voice. Hester was moving towards him, but before she could answer, he let the carbine fall to the ground and he put his arms out, held her firmly against his heaving chest.

'How did you know that we were here . . . that *I* was here?' she asked after a long time.

'I didn't. But I knew it was goin' to be here or hereabouts.'

Smollet made a small grunting sound and tried to raise himself. But all he could manage was a roll of his head as Burt stared coldly down at him.

'There must've been somethin' else,' he said, breathless from a cold, waxy face.

'I saw a little feller leavin'. Only thing known to see off a roadrunner's, the stink o' sheepmen,' Burt answered.

'Damn you, Lane. Why didn't Dodgson get to you?'

Burt shrugged. 'I don't know. But I think he might've tried,' he said. 'Right here's near enough to where it all started, Smollet, so it's fittin' it's where you die. At least it ain't behind them bars you're so scared of.'

Smollet's mouth formed the rictus of a smile. 'That's good. Nothin's all bad,' he grated. Then he shuddered and turned his face back to the dirt.

'You just might be an exception to that,' Burt responded.

24

Burt nodded towards the three horses that were huddled close at the end of the fault. 'Let's see about gettin' you out, before this place gets any fuller,' he said. 'We'll ride to where the creek bends west, then you ride on to the ranch. The place is bristlin' with friendly guns, so you'll be safe enough.'

'What are you goin' to do?' Hester asked, with distressing sentiment.

'I'll come back an' listen to Smollet's dyin' words,' Burt replied as they tightened the cinches of their horses.

'You already heard them. It's because you think Cole Dodgson's on his way here. If he is, are you goin' to kill him, too?'

'I tried not to kill Maber, but it was never goin' to work. I guess it'll be the same with Dodgson. If I do kill him, he'll be the only one to begrudge me.'

Hester weighed up her choices. 'I'm a newspaper-man's daughter, Burt, an' here's where the story is,' she asserted shortly. 'So I'll stay to the end, an' report your quarrel in *my* words.'

Burt rolled his eyes. 'OK, lady, but it's a tough way to win your spurs. An' if you don't do as I say, I'll send you out o' here trussed like a Thanksgivin' turkey.'

'Very thrilling. Perhaps you should write my headline,' Hester replied with a dry smile. Burt walked over to Smollet's body and took the Colt from the man's outstretched fingers. 'Here, take this,' he said, handing it to Hester. 'Get yourself back under that blanket, an' stay there. I'm goin' to keep an eye on the trail around this little hidey-hole. I need some warnin' of Dodgson gettin' here, an' I'm guessin' he won't be without help.'

'I'm ridin' north . . . buyin' an end o' line ticket on the Flyer,' Farrer rasped, as he and Dodgson drew their horses up to the pine stand.

'Well, before you go, you can tell me where the hell it is you've *been*,' Dodgson demanded. 'An' what the hell happened to Lane?'

Burt was standing in the sandstone cleft, deep in the shadow of the oak. He listened while the men sat their horses and talked. To him, it didn't sound like it was the first time that Dodgson had asked the question of Farrer.

'He never showed . . . not at the house,' Farrer said. 'I told you he weren't no pilgrim.'

'He's got to be out there somewhere,' Dodgson said in disbelief.

153

'He was out there all right. He was watchin'. I swung the lamp around so's he'd see it, but some goddamn, mad dogs got loose. You never told me about *them,*' Farrer snorted.

Burt sucked a mouthful of air through his teeth, swallowed a wicked snigger.

'I got in the house an' waited,' Farrer continued. 'Then the dogs ran off, an' I wasn't goin' to hang around and find out why. Just as well, 'cause that's when a bunch o' cowboys rode in.'

'So Lane *was* in town,' Dodgson said. 'Takin' the girl has upped the pot. Still, we're all out of harm's way here, an' it'll give me time to think.'

'I told you, I'm movin' on,' Farrer said decisively. 'There ain't much prospect in me an' you goin' up against the ranchers, the settlers, the law *an'* Burt Lane. It's so close to suicidal, I ain't even goin' to draw pay.'

Burt waited a moment for the gunshot that he thought Dodgson would retaliate with, but it never came, and he backtracked quietly. He looked around, saw that Hester was curled against the angle of the drift with the blanket around her. He wanted to cover her and positioned himself to one side of her motionless figure.

Cole Dodgson whistled an impatient signal of his arrival as he pushed his way unflinchingly into the fault. 'How are you all makin' out ... where's the girl?' he called out, not looking too closely at the features of the man standing in front of him. But the next moment, he jerked smartly on the reins, froze in his tracks.

The man before him wasn't Maber or Smollet. It was the deathly presence known as Burt Lane. Dodgson's heart thudded and his chest heaved as he saw the bodies of Smollet and Maber. There was no need for any explanation. Dodgson knew that it was Burt who'd killed them.

Then the cunning, the instinct for survival, overcame the grip of Dodgson's fear, and he nodded, went for the delaying tactic of a reconciled grin. At the same time, he let himself fall sideways from the saddle. The first bullet from Burt's carbine ripped close to the side of his head, but as he hit the ground he plainly heard an echo of his last thoughts.

'Finally get to meet all your worst fears, Dodgson,' Burt said as he fired a second time.

With a .45 bullet hammered into the top of one leg, Dodgson yelled, thrust himself up and forward on the other. He reached out for Hester, then clawed desperately for his Colt as he crumpled.

Hester screamed, then her own Colt boomed, the sound muffled by the heavy blanket and the closeness of Dodgson's body.

The sheepman's body jerked back into the air, where it collected another round from Burt's gun. Dodgson saw Burt advancing as his face piled into the shifting dirt of the drift. Pulling the trigger was his last move, and he didn't feel the pain as the bullet from his own gun drove deep into his belly.

155

'Even has to have a go at shootin' himself,' Burt said in a near whisper. As he reloaded, Hester kicked away the blanket. She got to her feet and stared fixedly at him, didn't let her gaze stray to the dead men.

'I could syndicate this story to the *Sheridan Examiner*,' she suggested impassively and dropped Smollet's Colt.

'Yeah, you do *that*, while I'm tellin' the folk of Clayburn that their sheep problem's over,' Burt responded with a touch of satisfaction. 'An' one o' them runnin' birds gets its home back, too,' he added.

Burt and Hester were sitting their horses at the south fork of Gray Bull Creek. Burt was holding the reins of the spare mount, a rimrock mare that had been stolen by the sheepmen from Ruse Barrow's farm.

'Are you sure about Smollet? That he was one of those men who were here before?' Hester asked, careful that she didn't sound reproving in any way.

'He was a sheepman. A sheepman who was just about to snuff me *an'* you out. *That's* enough to be sure of,' he answered brusquely. 'Let's just get back to Wild Meddow.'

25

The day was closing fast as Burt and Hester rode towards the home pasture of Wild Meddow. In the yard, men and horses were milling around a campfire that brightened up first dark.

From the house, yellow lamplight glowed from a window and the open front door.

'My home's lookin' like a popular place to be. With a pianola turnin', it could be mistaken for Lefty Dete's,' Burt said drily.

'Hmm,' Hester agreed. 'Let's hope the clientele's as welcoming.'

Burt gave a whistle and shouted, laughed at the outbreak of keyed-up barking.

Since the two of them had emerged from the creekside timber, a group of men had been watching their approach. Set to forestall trouble, Brewster Carron and his cowboys moved apart. But it wasn't long before one of them let out a whoop and hurried forward.

'Hey Lane, is that you? Miss Hester, too?' the Ankle Iron man hollered.

Burt and Hester laughed. 'Yeah, it's the both of us,' Burt shouted back. 'Couldn't stay away longer.' He raised a hand in greeting to Carron. 'We'd appreciate you'd sendin' a rider to Clayburn, fast,' he said. 'Get word to Hester's pa, an' ask the marshal if he can send out a man with a shovel. The buzzards'll show him where to go.'

'Hey Burton! If you'd stayed away any longer, I'd have gained myself another outfit. Now, I've got to show appreciation for nothin',' a voice boomed out cheerfully.

Burt turned from the cowboys to see Noble Rockford standing in the doorway of his house. 'Ha, glad you think it's as much as an *outfit*,' he returned. 'What the hell brought you down here?'

'Milo mentioned you was in a spot o' trouble.' Rockford took off his hat, nodded and smiled his introduction to Hester. 'We got hold of a bunch o' stubble jumpers. Missed the big daddies, though.'

'That's 'cause I've been takin' care of 'em. There should be more to life than switchin' a besom,' Burt said. He let go the reins of the mare and swung tiredly down from the saddle.

'You start out thinkin' that,' Rockford responded. 'But you've probably got more domestic type chores ahead o' you.'

'Uh huh,' Burt coughed, the inference not escaping him. 'So, where's all my mutts?' he shouted.

158

Hester walked her horse alongside Burt. 'Bein' here's fine, but I do need to get back to town,' she said. 'I've decided I *am* writin' this story. An' I *will* try to syndicate it.'

'Good. Is that why you asked about Texas Smollet?' Burt asked.

'Yes. Pa says to print the fact, when you can. Well, to start off with, an' as long as it doesn't spoil your story. It's the yardstick for all his editor's jokes.'

Burt smiled broadly as he kneeled to gently pummel his dogs. 'I'll ride in with you. I think it's time I told your pa somethin' . . . or ask him. I'm not sure which,' he said. Then he cursed, as one of the pups sank its sharp teeth into the flesh of his hand.